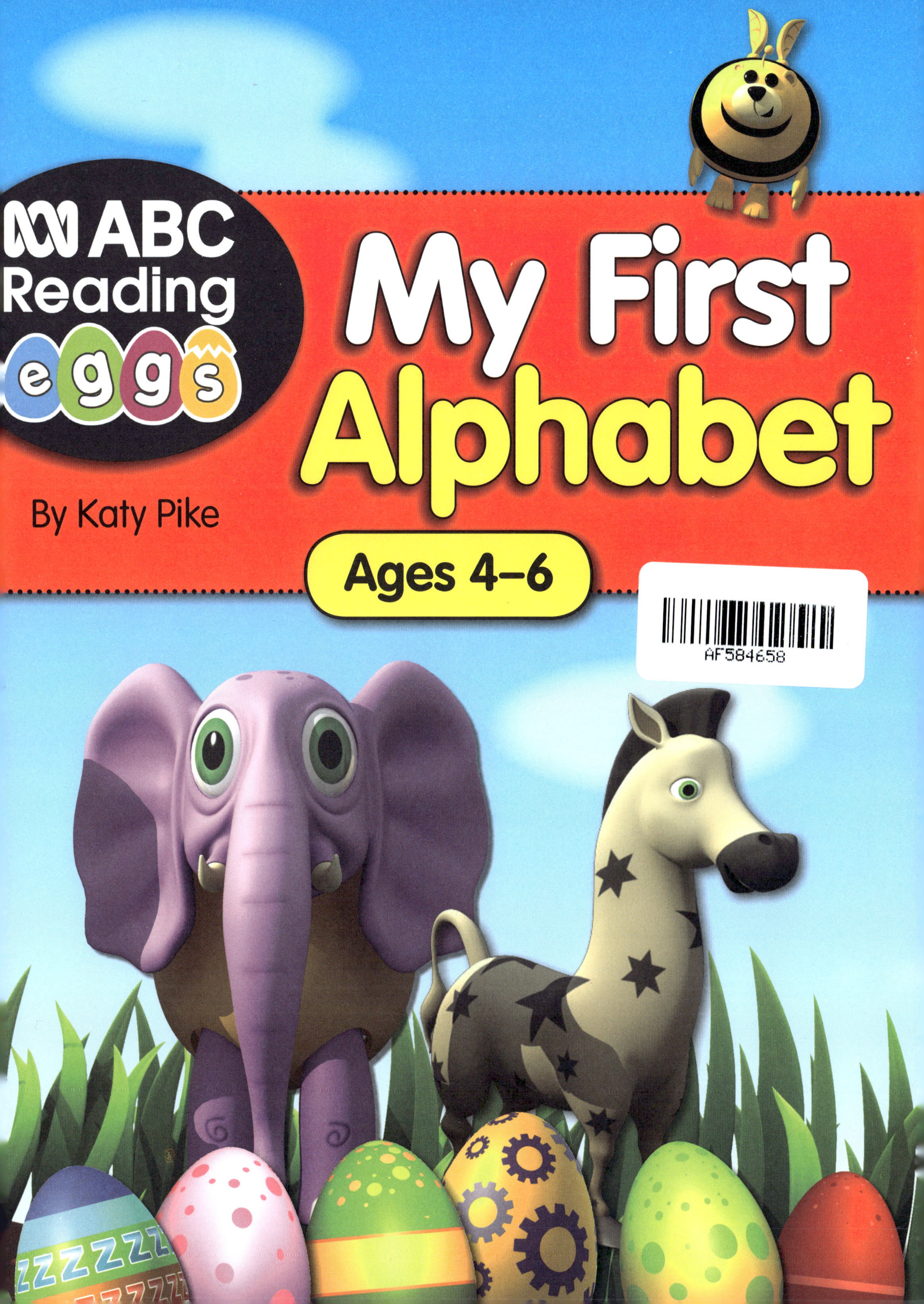
ABC Reading eggs
My First Alphabet
By Katy Pike
Ages 4–6

Dear Parent or Carer,

This book is part of the **My First** series of **Reading Eggs** workbooks. **Reading Eggs** has proven to be very popular with parents, children and teachers. The **Reading Eggs** books and website have helped more than 20 million children worldwide learn to read.

Each vibrant book in the **My First** series includes a wide range of interesting activities that will help your child develop essential reading and writing skills. Written by experienced teachers and educators, the series supports what your child learns at school.

The pages are clear and uncluttered, with activities that build real skills. Activities are fun and motivate children to continue working and learning. Instructions are easy to follow and regular challenges entice children to extend their learning.

I hope that you and your child enjoy using this and other books in the series.

Kind regards, Katy Pike
Publisher

ABC Reading Eggs My First Alphabet

ISBN: 978-1-74215-162-5

Reprinted 2012, 2013, 2014, 2015, 2016, 2018, 2019, 2020, 2021, 2022, 2023, 2024, 2025

Distributed by:
Pascal Press
PO Box 250
Glebe NSW 2037

www.readingeggs.com
Written by Katy Pike
Publisher: Katy Pike
Editors: Sandra Iannella and Amanda Santamaria
Design and layout by Modern Art Production Group
Printed in China by 1010 Printing International Ltd

Contents

Alphabet activities to do at home

Focus on the letter sound

The name of the letter is important but for children learning to read, knowing the sound the letter makes is highly useful. When working with letters, try to accent the sound of the letter, eg the letter Bee says 'b' as in ball.

How many?

Focusing on one letter at a time, try to think up as many words as you can that begin with that letter. Do this together as a family and see how many words you can find for each letter. You can even make your own *Family Alphabet Book*. Write a new letter on each page and list all the words you can think of for each letter.

Sing the ABC song

This all-time favourite is a great way to begin to learn the letters and their place in the alphabet. "Now I know my ABC, won't you come and sing with me?"

Make flashcards

Use flashcards or make your own with one letter on each card. Make a full set of cards using all capital and lower-case letters; that's 52 cards in all. Your child can: decorate the cards; practise naming each letter and the sound it makes; match capital and lower-case letters, eg A with a, B with b etc; put them in alphabetical order using the alphabet song to help them.

A

a

Reading Eggs Alphabet flashcards

Use the **Reading Eggs** Alphabet flashcards and play the games in the pack to build letter recognition and letter sounds.

Rainbow letters

Draw a large letter in the centre of an A4 sheet of paper. Ask your child to trace the letter using different coloured pencils or crayons to create a rainbow letter.

An alphabet of animals

If your child likes animals, use books, encyclopaedias or the Internet to find an animal or animals for every letter of the alphabet. Make your own *Alphabet of Animals* book.

An ABC of food

You could repeat the Alphabet of Animals activity with food. Find a food for each letter of the alphabet.

Playdough alphabet

Use playdough to make each letter shape. It's fun and you can move onto short words or your child's name. Decorate each letter to look like something that starts with that letter, such as adding a leaf to the letter a to make it look like an apple; ears on the letter c for cat; and a cute puppy face on the ball of the d for a dog with its tail in the air.

Pipe-cleaners

Pipe-cleaners and other bendy craft materials are a great resource for working with letters. You can make the letters, create words, stick them onto cards and have lots of fun.

Magnetic letters

Magnetic fridge letters can be great fun for all the family. You can put them in order, pull one out and ask which one is missing. Write simple words and messages to each other. Make it part of your daily routine at breakfast or dinner, focusing on a new letter or word each time. Magnetic letters are a great way to play with letters and words on a daily basis.

Name that thing

Look at things at home and when you're out and about, and ask your child to name them. See if they can tell you what sound the word begins with. If they can't, help them and in time they will take over. When they get really good at this, you can replace the beginning sound with the end sound. What sound does the word end with?

Alphabet chart

Dd
Dogfin

Ee
Eggyphant

Ff
Frogfish

Jj
Jelly Jag

Kk
Kangako

Ll
Lemon Lizard

Pp
Pinkipoo

Qq
Queenie Quail

Rr
Red Rabbit

Vv
Village Van

Ww
Wheely Whale

Xx
Xpanda

Zz
Zebstar

Aa

A is for Appley Ant.

1 Trace and write.

2 Circle every A.

A B A E S

T A N A A

How many? ____

Circle every a.

a c n a g

c a o a a

How many? ____

3 Add a and then say the word.

a pple

____nt

____rrow

____stronaut

4 Circle the apples that begin with **a**.

5 Match each letter to a picture.

a
f
a
s
a

sun

CHALLENGE

How many ants can you draw here?
4 Good! 7 Great!!
10 Excellent!!!

Bb

Buzz, buzz!
I'm Bee Bee Bear.

1 Trace and write.

2 Circle every B.

B A P B C

B A O R B

How many? ____

Circle every b.

b b d p b

a b e b g

How many? ____

3 Add b and then say the word.

b ee

____ ear

____ all

____ ook

4 Circle the bubbles that begin with b.

5 Match each letter to a picture.

b
a
b
o
b

CHALLENGE

How many beads can you draw on the string?

6 Good! 8 Great!! 10 Excellent!!!

1 **Trace and write.**

C ______ c ______

2 **Circle every C.**

C C C A C
B O C D G

How many? ______

Circle every c.

c a o c c
b c c a c

How many? ______

3 **Add c and then say the word.**

______at

______amel

______oat

______arrot

4 Circle the jigsaw parts that begin with c.

5 Match each letter to a picture.

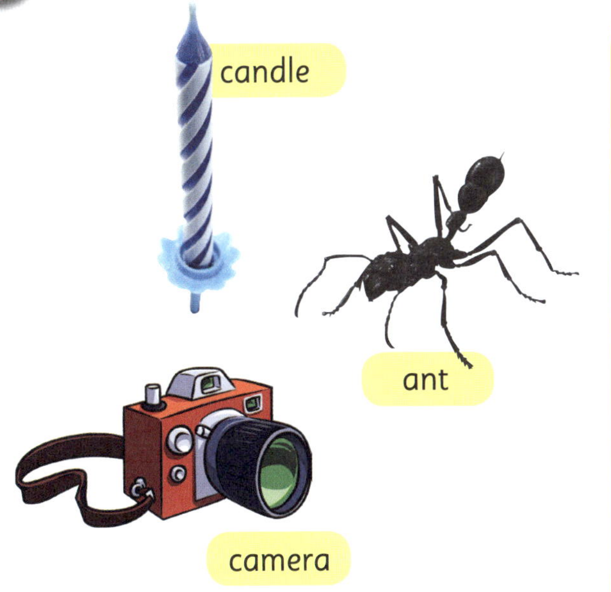

c
b
c
a
c
m

CHALLENGE

How many colours can you name?
4 Good! 6 Great!! 8 Excellent!!!

Dd

1 Trace and write.

2 Circle every D.

D D A D D
C D B O J

How many? ____

Circle every d.

d c d d c
d a e b d

How many? ____

3 Add d and then say the word.

d og

____ olphin

____ uck

____ oor

4 Circle the doughnuts that begin with d.

5 Match each letter to a picture.

d
c
d
a
c

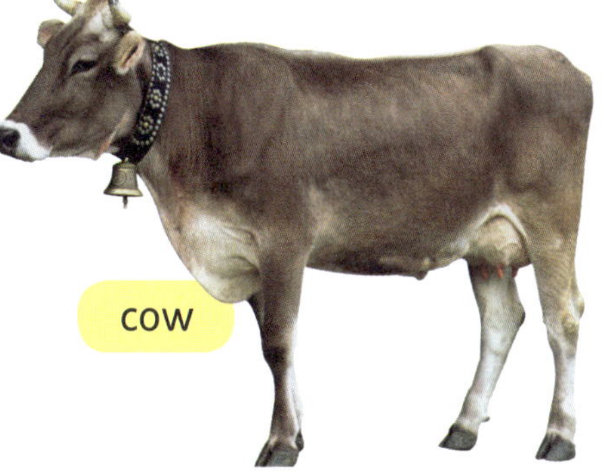

CHALLENGE Draw the dots on the dice.
3 Good! 4 Great!! 6 Excellent!!!

1 dot 2 dots 3 dots 4 dots 5 dots 6 dots

Find the hidden pictures

Find each drawing in the picture.

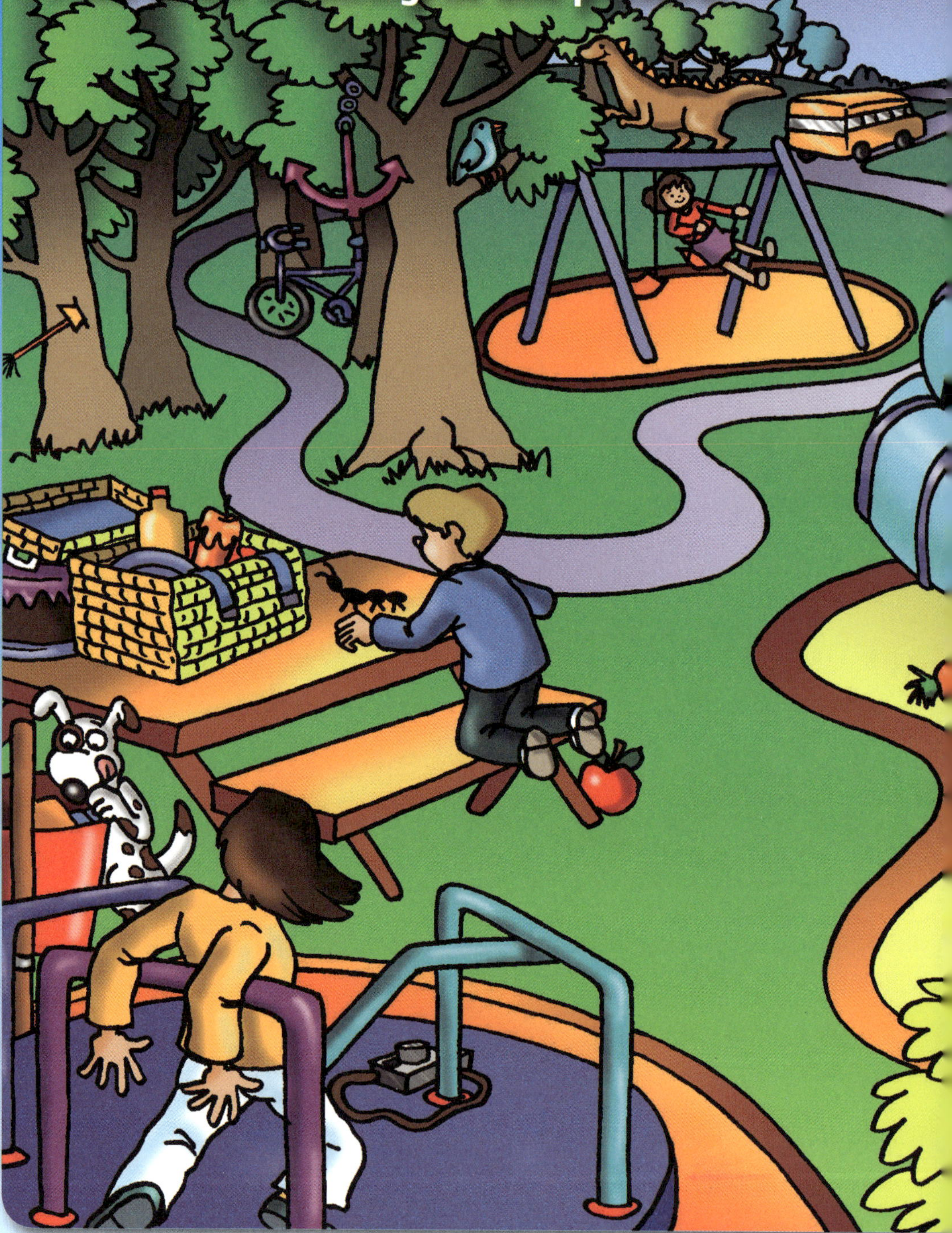

Aa

apple

ant

alien

anchor

ambulance

arrow

Bb

bee

bird

butterfly

bicycle

bus

balloon

basket

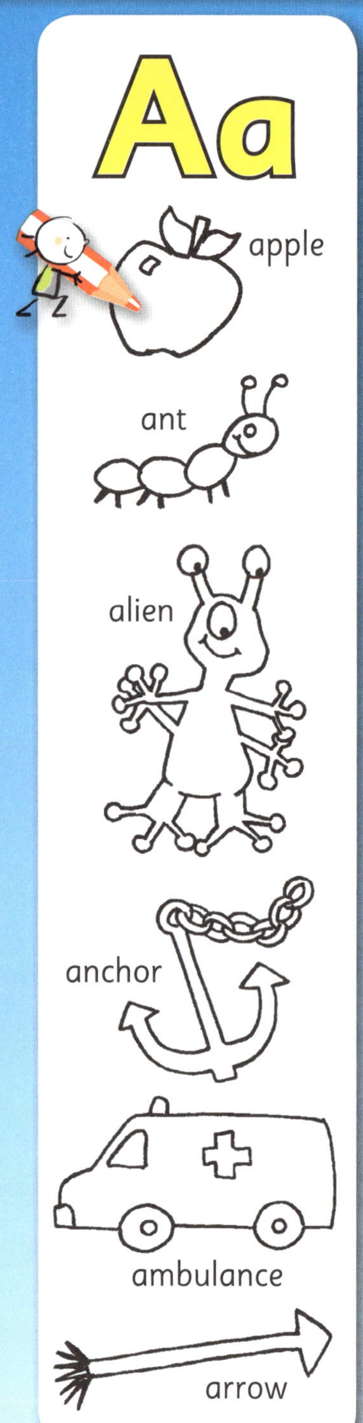

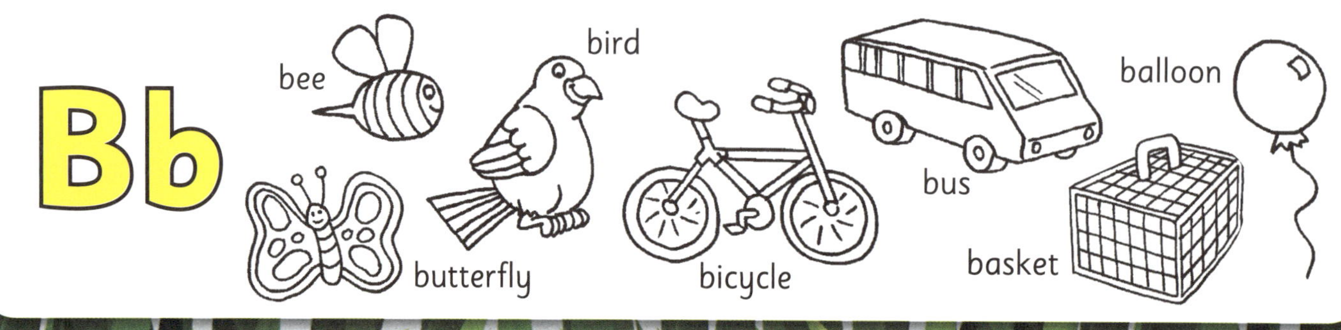

Dd
dinosaur
dice
dog
duck
doll

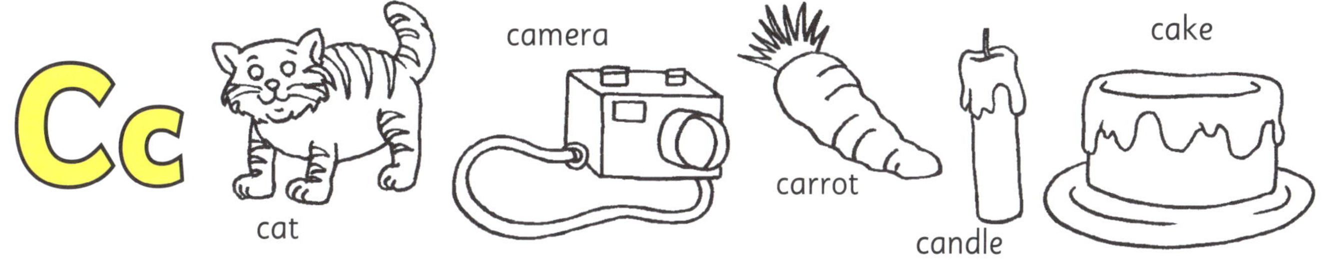
Cc
cat
camera
carrot
candle
cake

Ee

1 Trace and write.

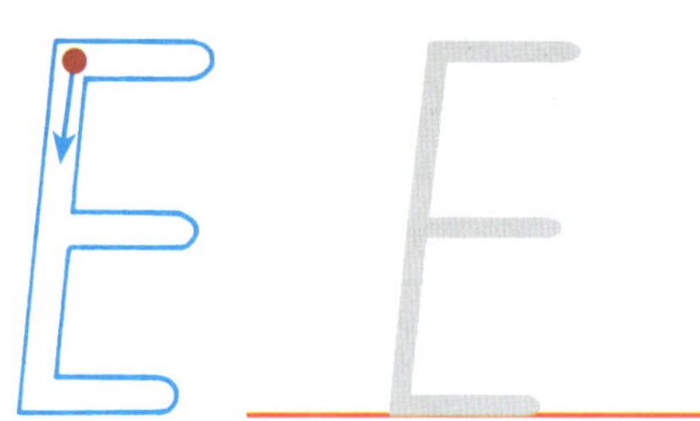

2 Circle every **E**.

E E E F R

C D E I E

How many? ____

Circle every **e**.

e b c e e

a e e o e

How many? ____

3 Add **e** and then say the word.

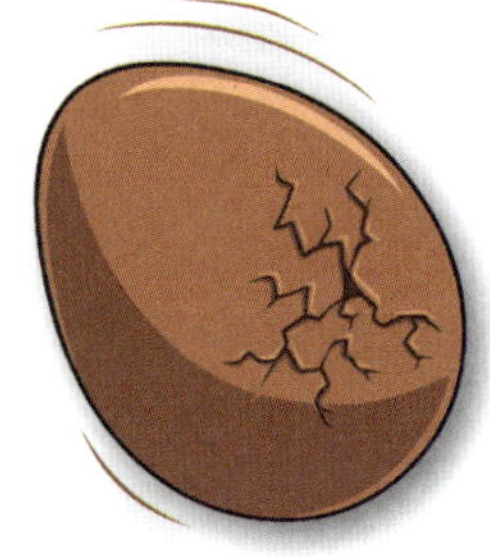

____gg

____lephant

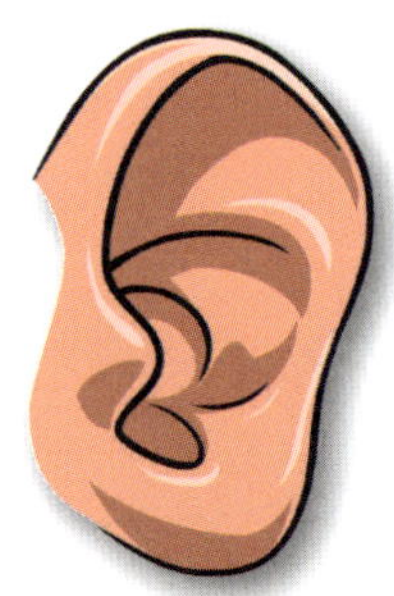

____ar

____at

4 Circle the eggs that begin with **e**.

5 Match each letter to a picture.

e
b
e
c
e

CHALLENGE

How many eggs can you draw here?
5 Good! 7 Great!!
10 Excellent!!!

1 Trace and write.

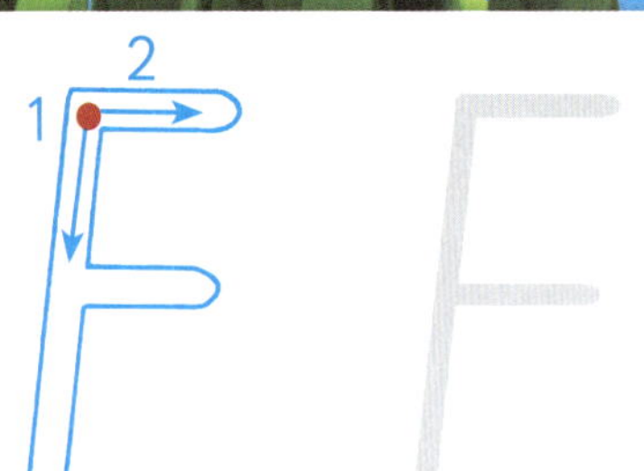

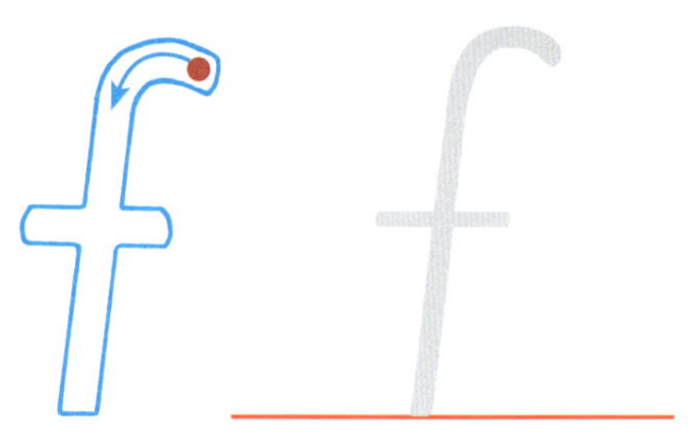

2 Circle every F.

F F E F Z
B F C A F

How many? ____

Circle every f.

f i f f f
f j l t f

How many? ____

3 Add f and then say the word.

f rog

____ ish

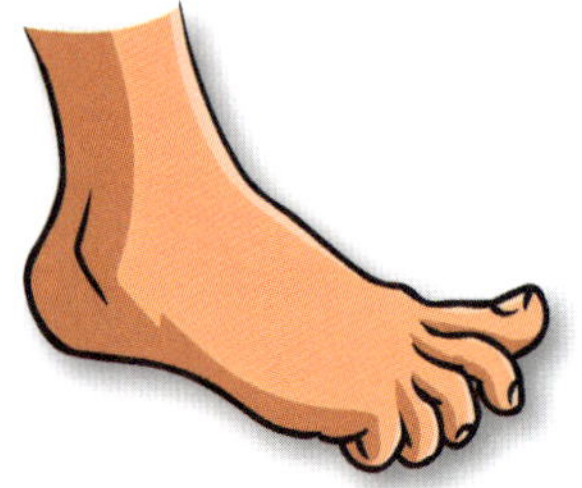

____ oot

____ ly

4 **Draw funny faces on all the fish.**

5 **Match each letter to a picture.**

f
e
f
d
f
c

CHALLENGE

How many fruits can you name?

4 Good! 8 Great!! 12 Excellent!!!

1 Trace and write.

G G g g

2 Circle every **G**.

G D G G C
G C G Q G

How many? ____

Circle every **g**.

g g g y g
j b g a g

How many? ____

3 Add **g** and then say the word.

g irl

____ uitar

____ oose

____ host

4 Circle the glasses that begin with g.

5 Match each letter to a picture.

g
a
g
c
b
g

CHALLENGE

How many green things can you think of?

5 Good! 8 Great!! 12 Excellent!!!

Hh

Hello, I'm Horse Hee Heepo.

1 Trace and write.

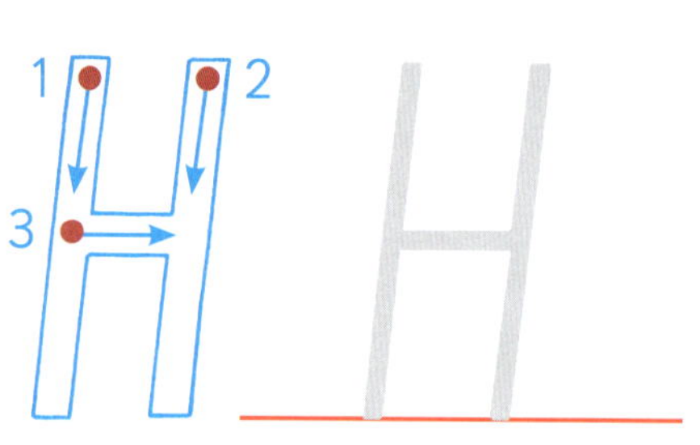

2 Circle every **H**.

H H H N T
I J H H H

How many? ____

Circle every **h**.

h m h t h
h n o h y

How many? ____

3 Add **h** and then say the word.

h orse

____ at

____ en

____ ut

4 Circle the jigsaw parts that begin with h.

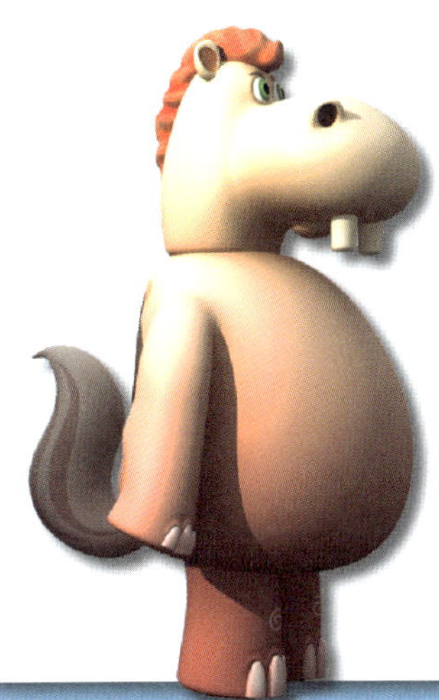

5 Match each letter to a picture.

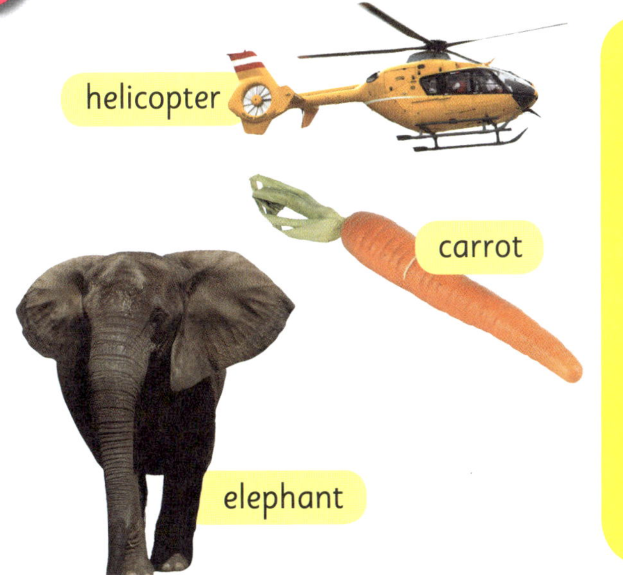

h
e
h
c
h

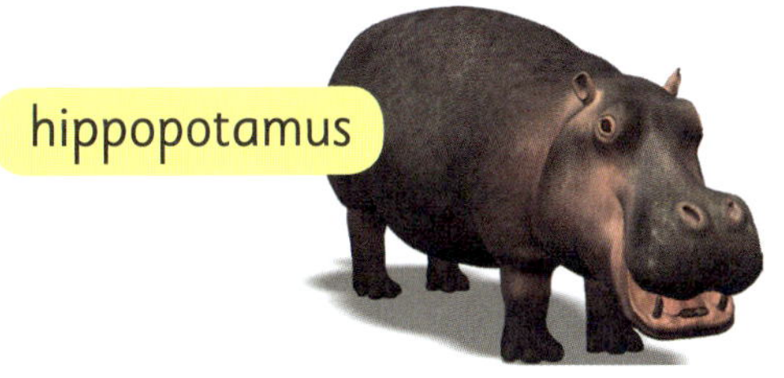

CHALLENGE Draw a different hairstyle on each head.
3 Good! 4 Great!! 6 Excellent!!!

 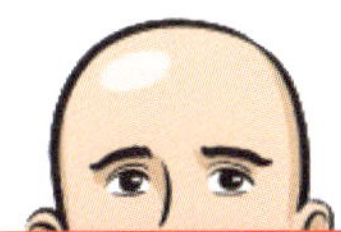 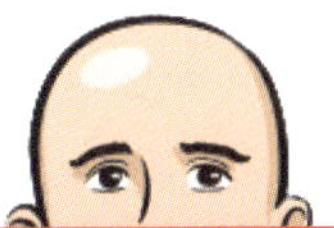   

Find the hidden pictures

Find each drawing in the picture.

Ee

egg

elephant

ear

elbow

exit

engine

Ff

fish

fly

feather

frog

flower

foot

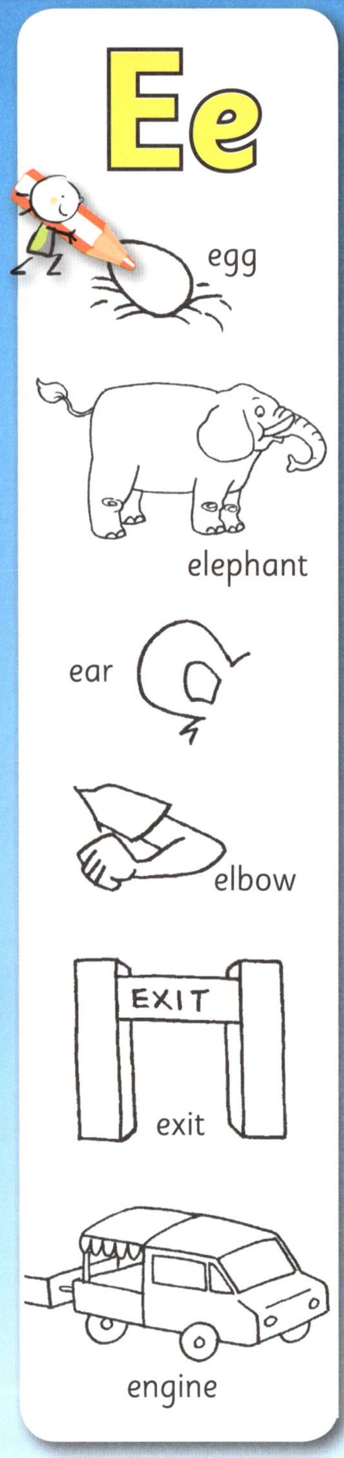

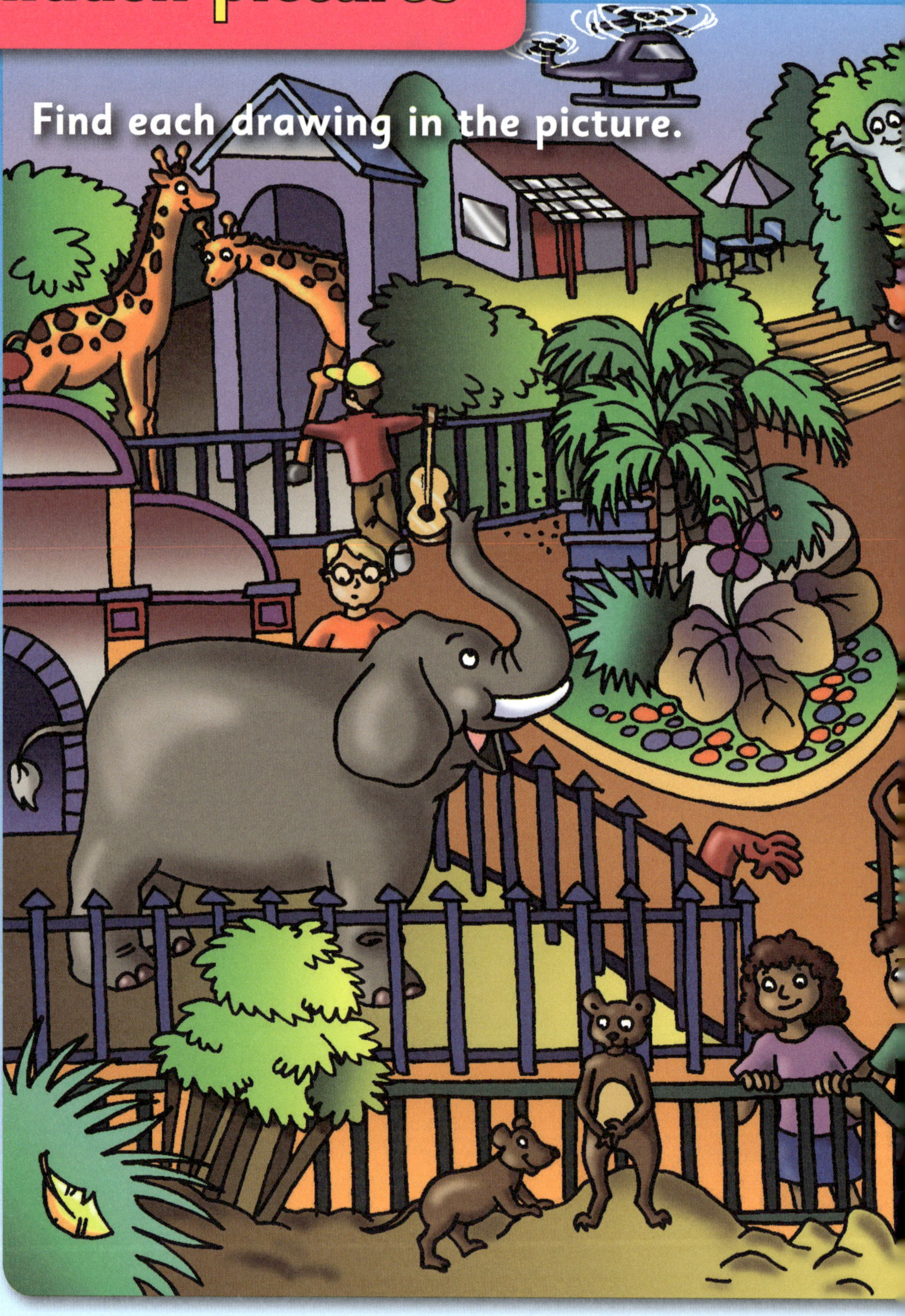

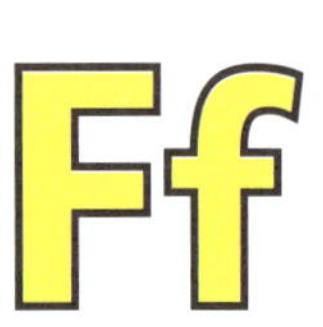

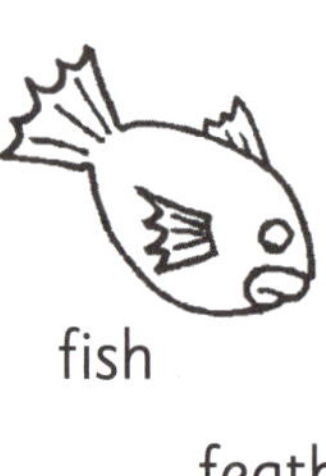

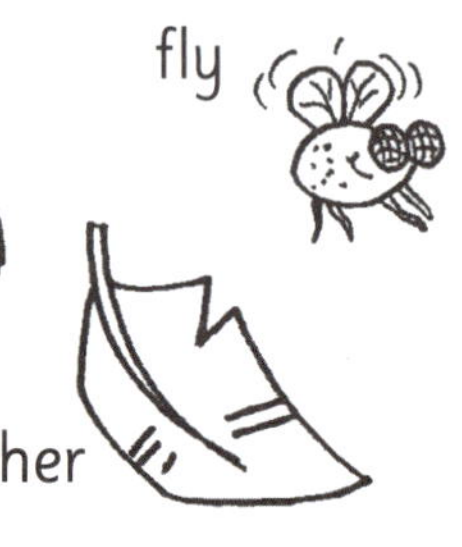

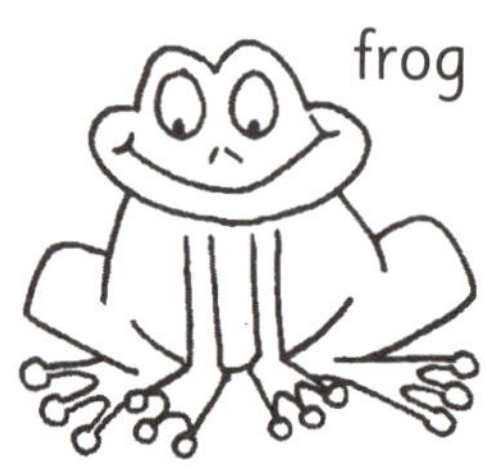

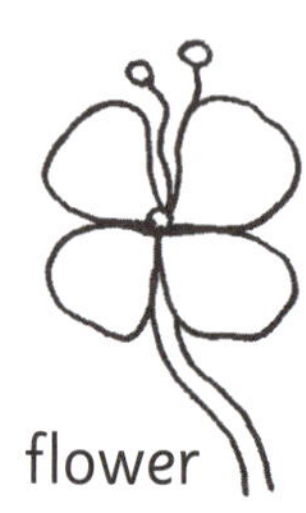

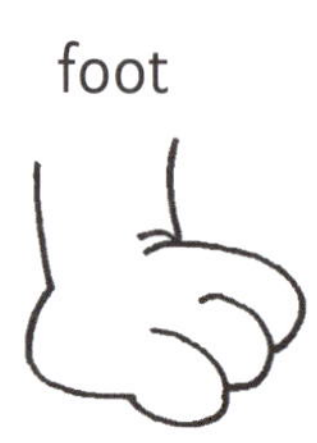

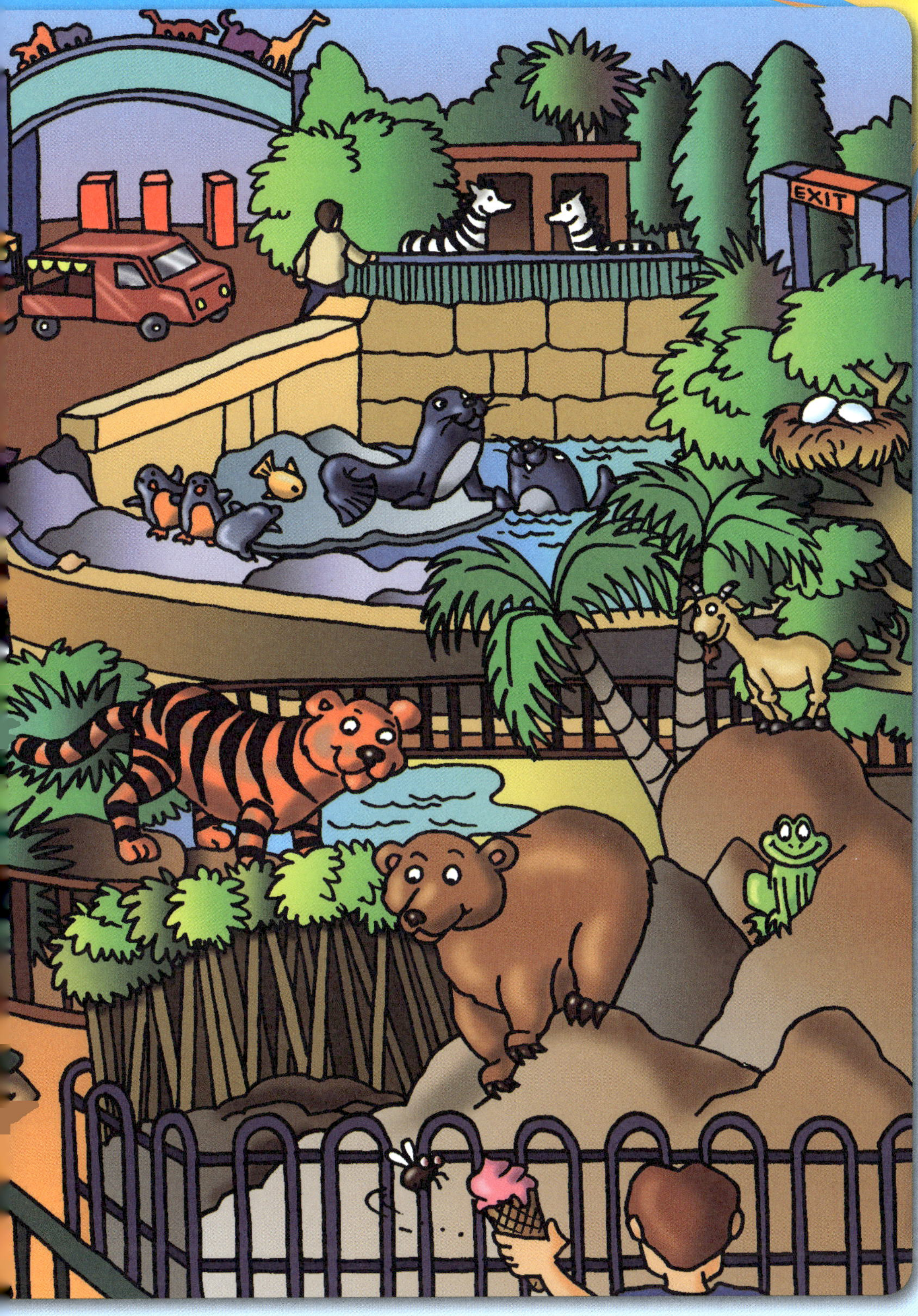
EXIT

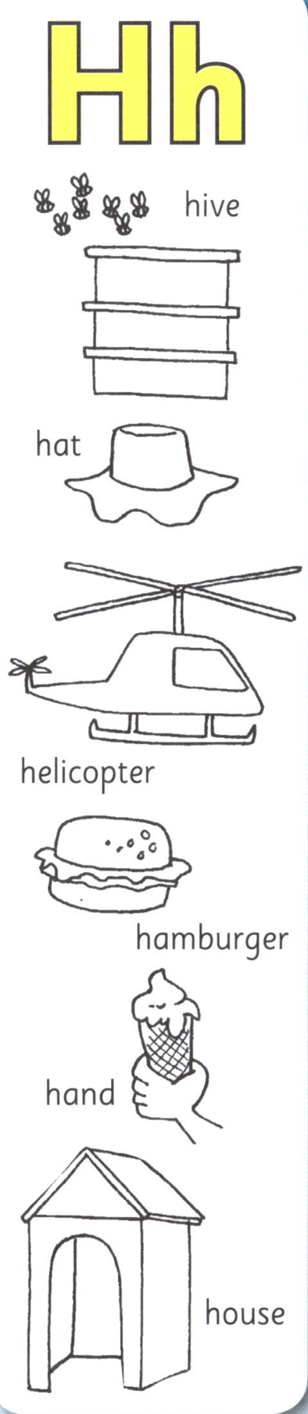

Hh

hive
hat
helicopter
hamburger
hand
house

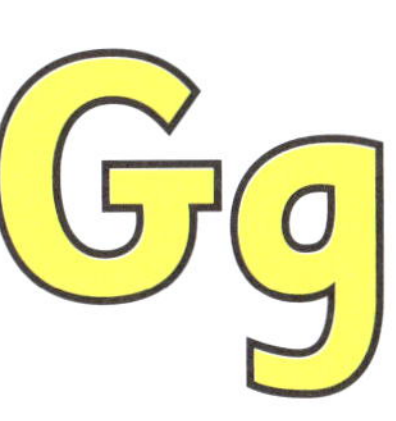

Gg

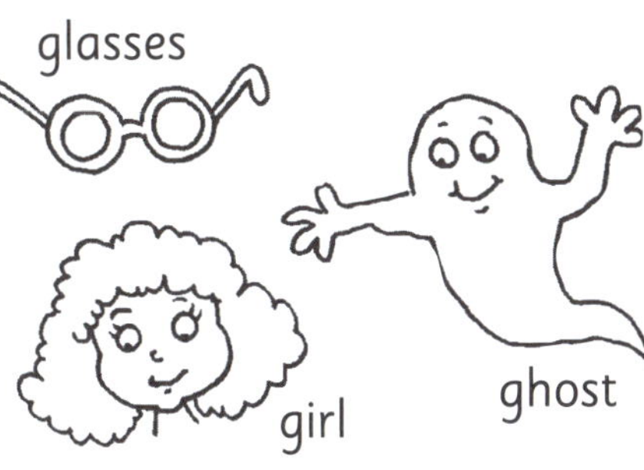

glasses
girl
ghost
goat
glove
guitar

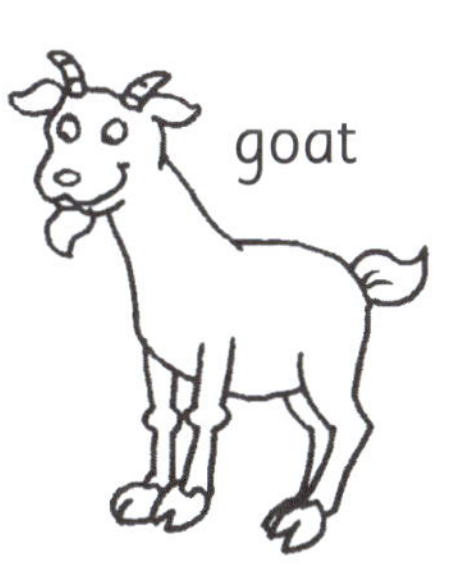

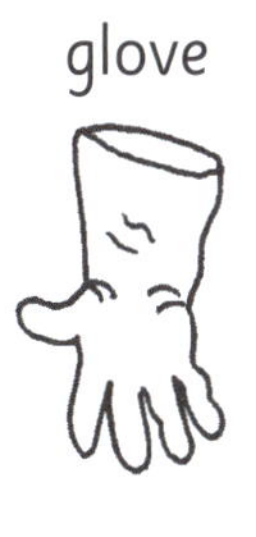

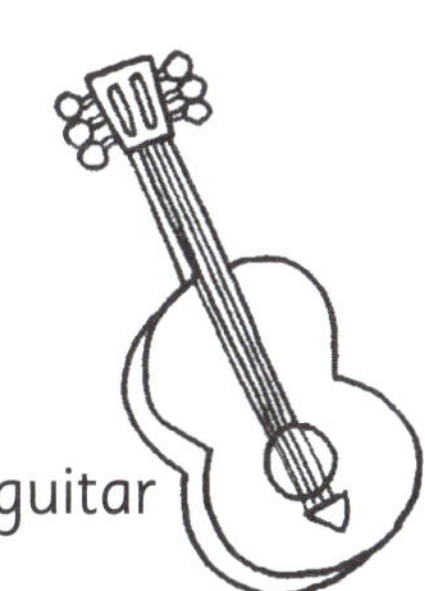

Ii

I is for Insillysect.

1 Trace and write.

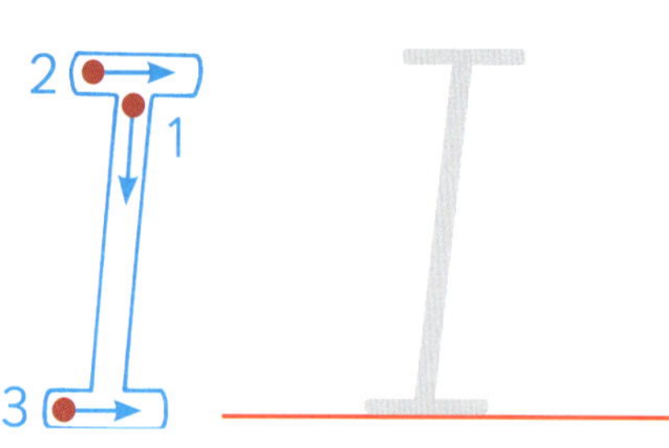

2 Circle every I.

I N I L I
I T J I V

How many? ____

Circle every i.

i i t i i
k i l j i

How many? ____

3 Add i and then say the word.

____ce

____nsects

____ce-cream

____nternet

4 Circle the ice-creams that begin with i.

5 Match each letter to a picture.

itch

island

i
b
i
h
i

basket

hamburger

invitation

CHALLENGE Draw ice-creams. How many flavours?
3 Good! 5 Great!! 7 Excellent!!!

J is for Jelly Jag.

1 Trace and write.

2 Circle every J.

J I J G C

J L Y J J

How many? ____

Circle every j.

j j j g j

i y j j b

How many? ____

3 Add j and then say the word.

____et

____eans

____ar

____uggle

4 Circle the jigsaw parts that begin with j.

5 Match each letter to a picture.

j
b
j
c
i

CHALLENGE

How many people can you tell this joke to?

Q: Why did the jellybean go to school?

A: Because he wanted to be a smartie!

2 Good! 3 Great!! 5 Excellent!!!

Kk

Hello, I'm Kangako.

1 Trace and write.

2 Circle every K.

K k K N K

H L K I E

How many? ____

Circle every k.

k k k k w

l r d k k

How many? ____

3 Add k and then say the word.

k angaroo

____ oala

____ ey

____ iss

4 Circle the kites that begin with k.

5 Match each letter to a picture.

k
a
k
e
k

CHALLENGE How many kites can you draw and colour?
2 Good! 3 Great!! 5 Excellent!!!

Ll

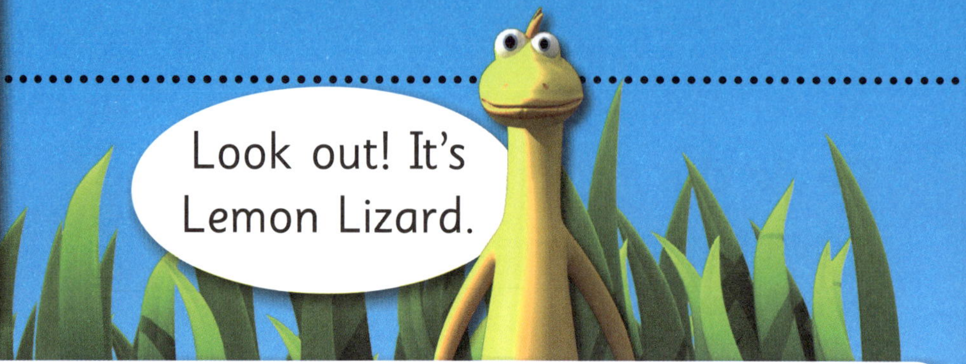

Look out! It's Lemon Lizard.

1 Trace and write.

L L l l

2 Circle every **L**.

L N E F L

L L L I J

How many? ____

Circle every **l**.

l n (t f

l i l l l

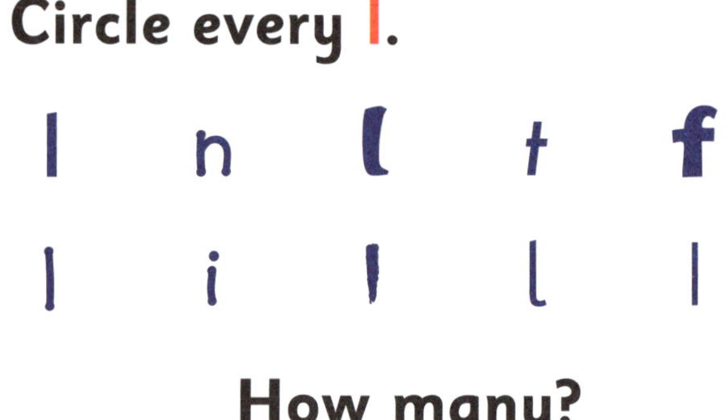

How many? ____

3 Add **l** and then say the word.

___emon

___izard

___eg

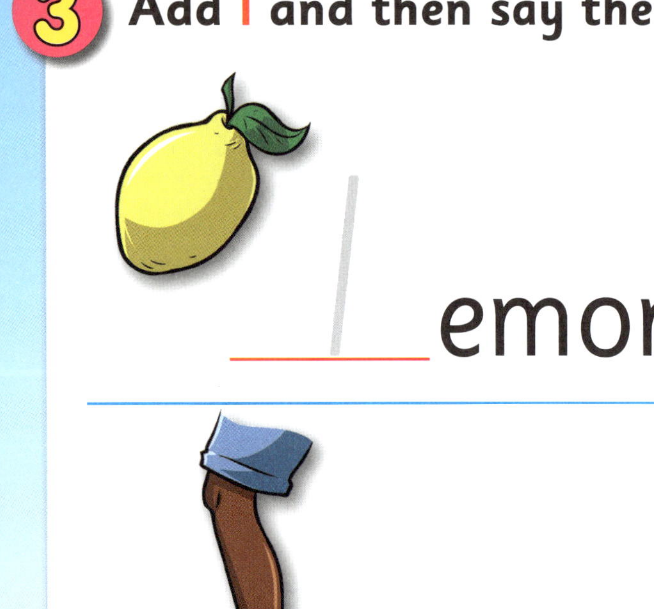

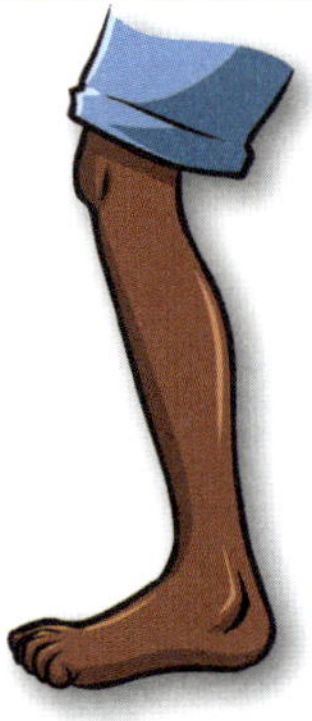

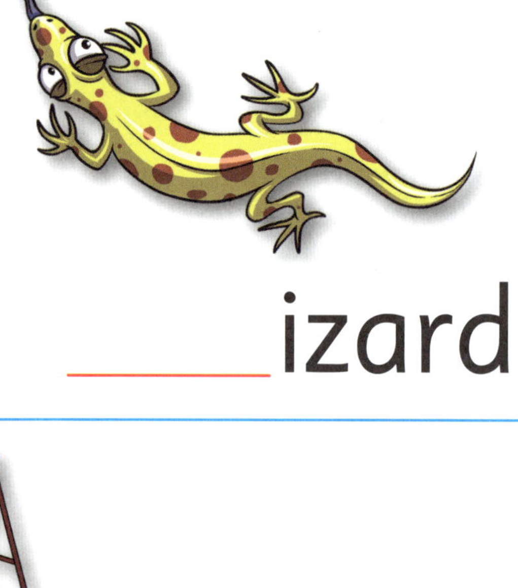

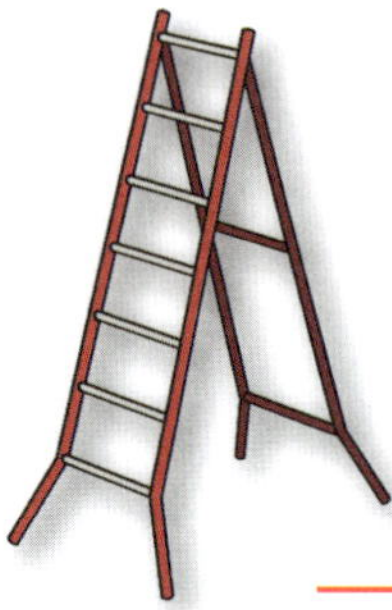

___adder

4 Circle the jigsaw parts that begin with l.

5 Match each letter to a picture.

l
k
l
b
l
e

CHALLENGE
How many more lines can you draw? 8 Good! 11 Great!! 15 Excellent!!!

Mm

Hello, I'm Marshmallow Mouse.

1 **Trace and write.**

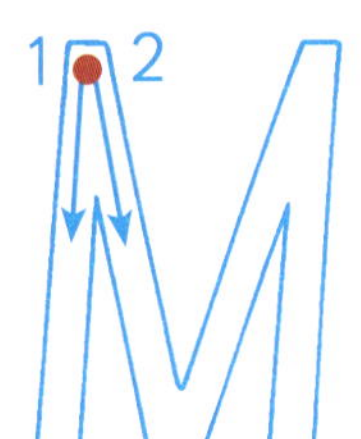

M M m m

2 **Circle every M.**

M E m R M
D M F M Z

How many? ____

Circle every m.

m h m n y
m k p m m

How many? ____

3 **Add m and then say the word.**

m an

____ ouse

____ onkey

____ oon

4 Circle the marshmallows that begin with m.

5 Match each letter to a picture.

l
m
d
m
a
m

CHALLENGE

How many foods can you think of that start with m?

3 Good! 5 Great!! 8 Excellent!!!

Find the hidden pictures

Find each drawing in the picture.

Ii

ice

ice-cream

insects

Jj

jug

juice

jet

Kk

kangaroo

kite

kitten

key

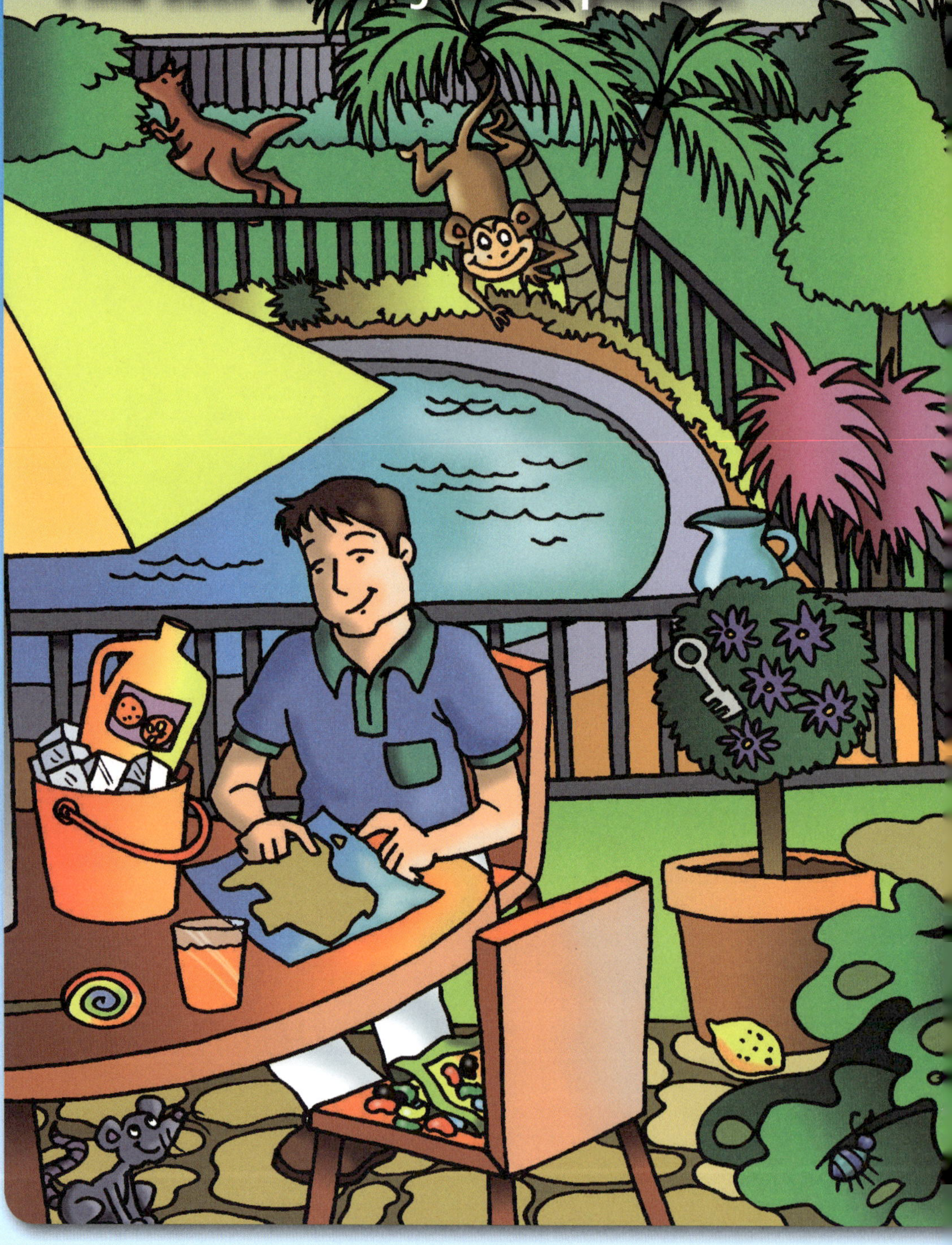

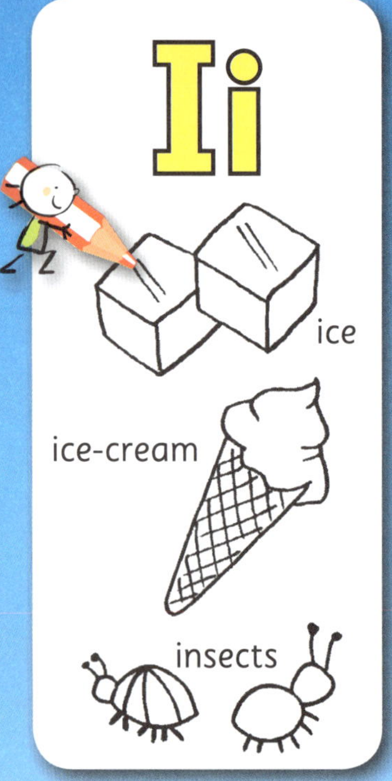

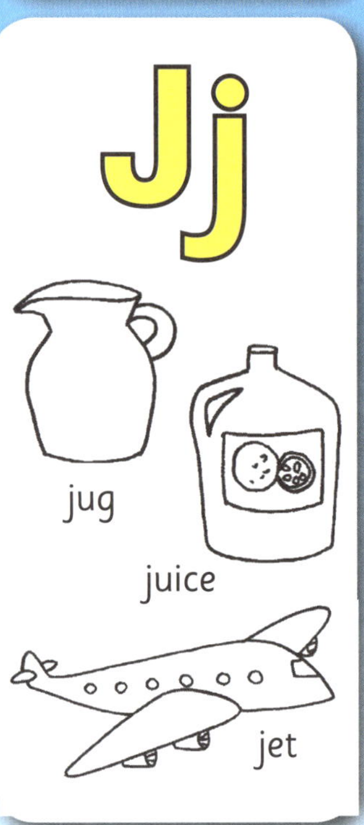

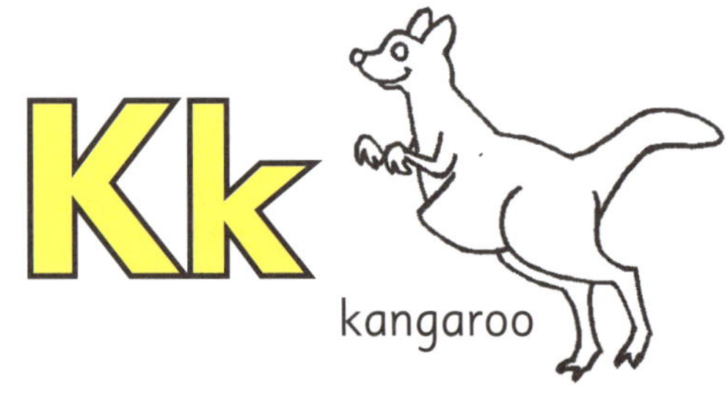

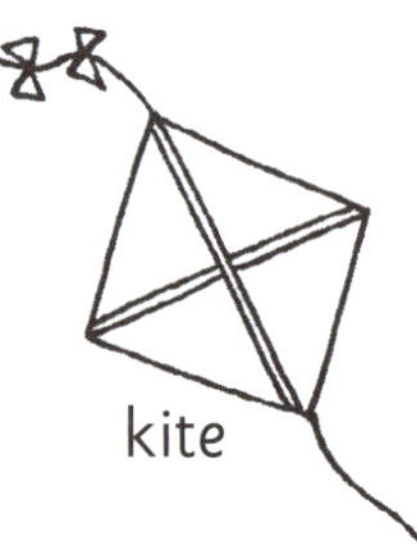

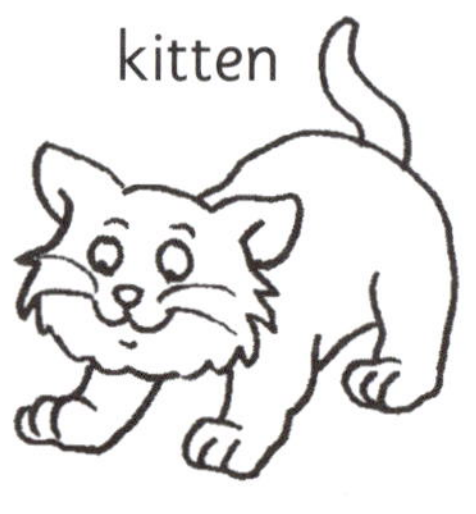

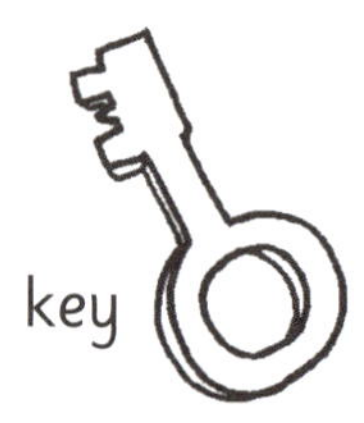

MILK

Mm

milk
MILK
mouse
monkey
man
map

Ll

lemon
lizard
ladybug
log
lollipop
ladder

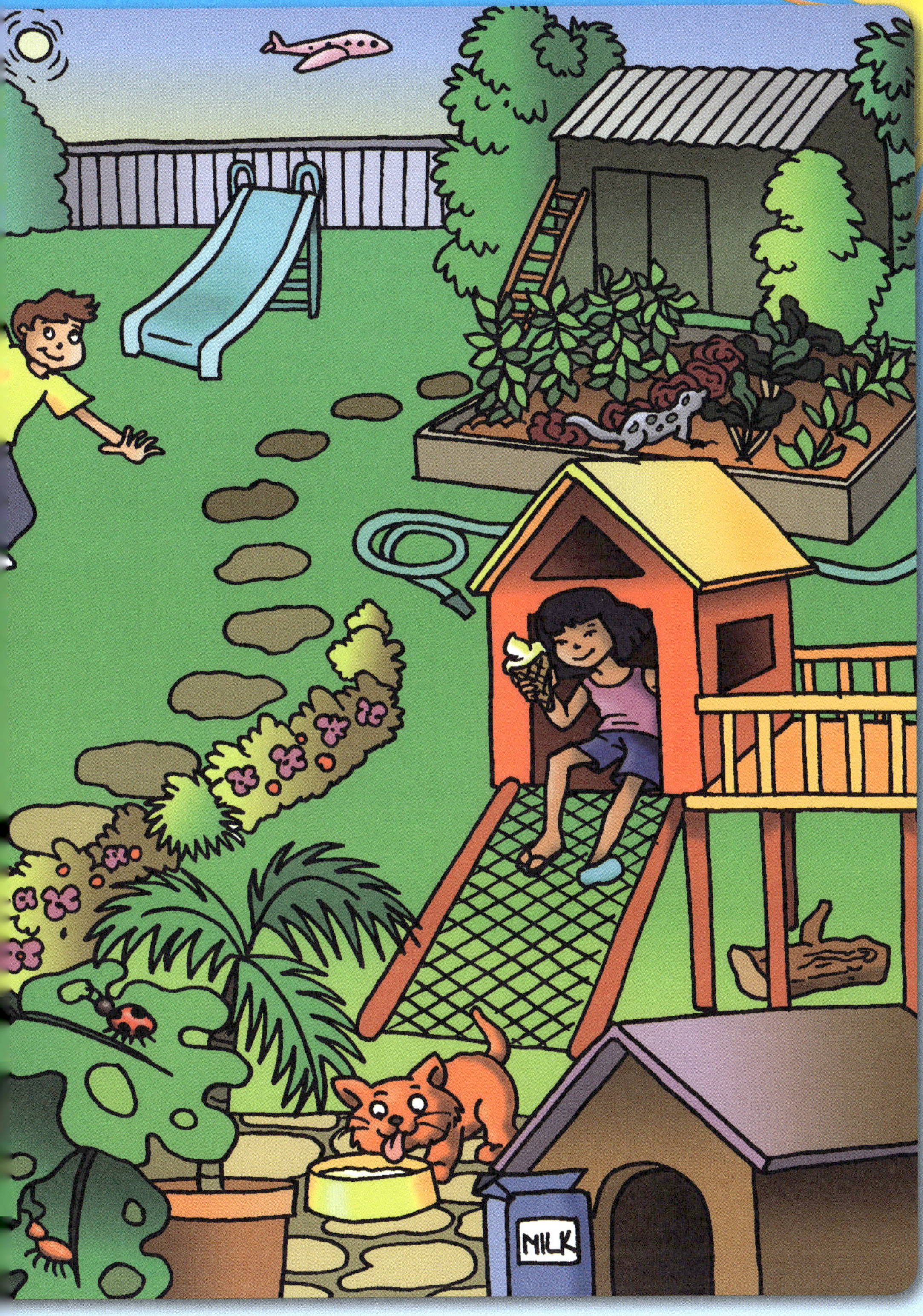

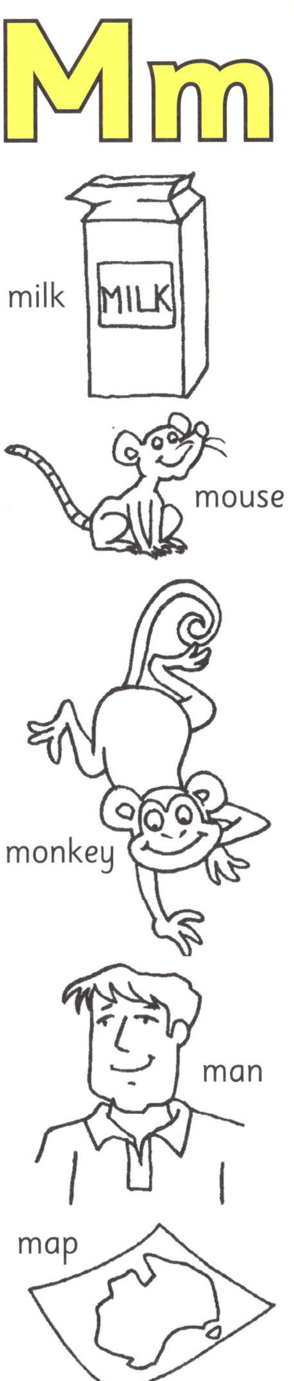

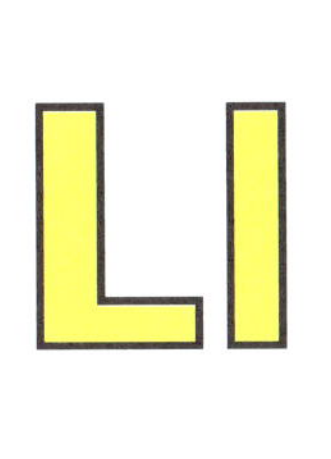

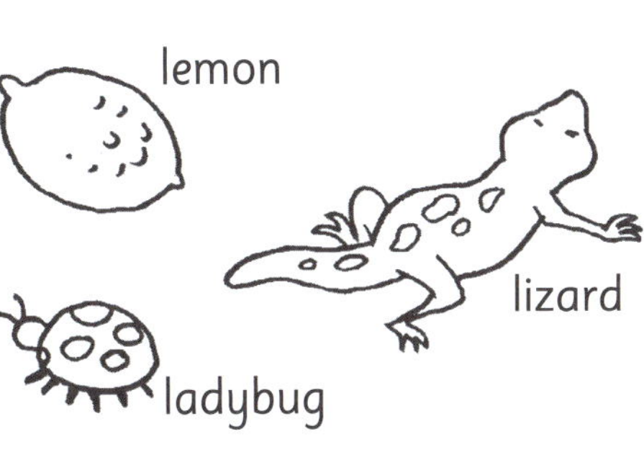

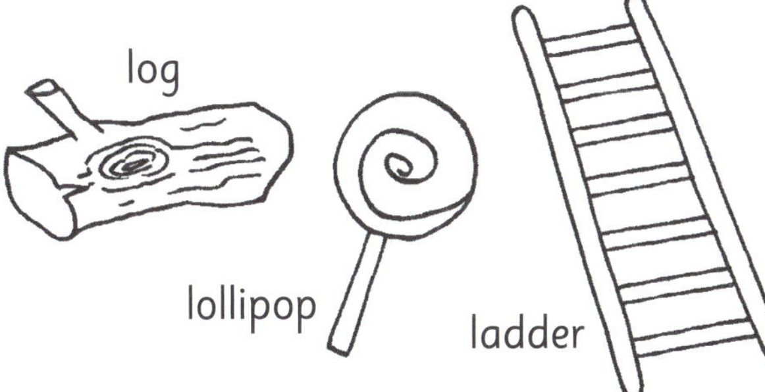

Dot-to-dots

Connect the dots from a to m.

a b c d e f g h i j k l m

Connect the dots from A to M.

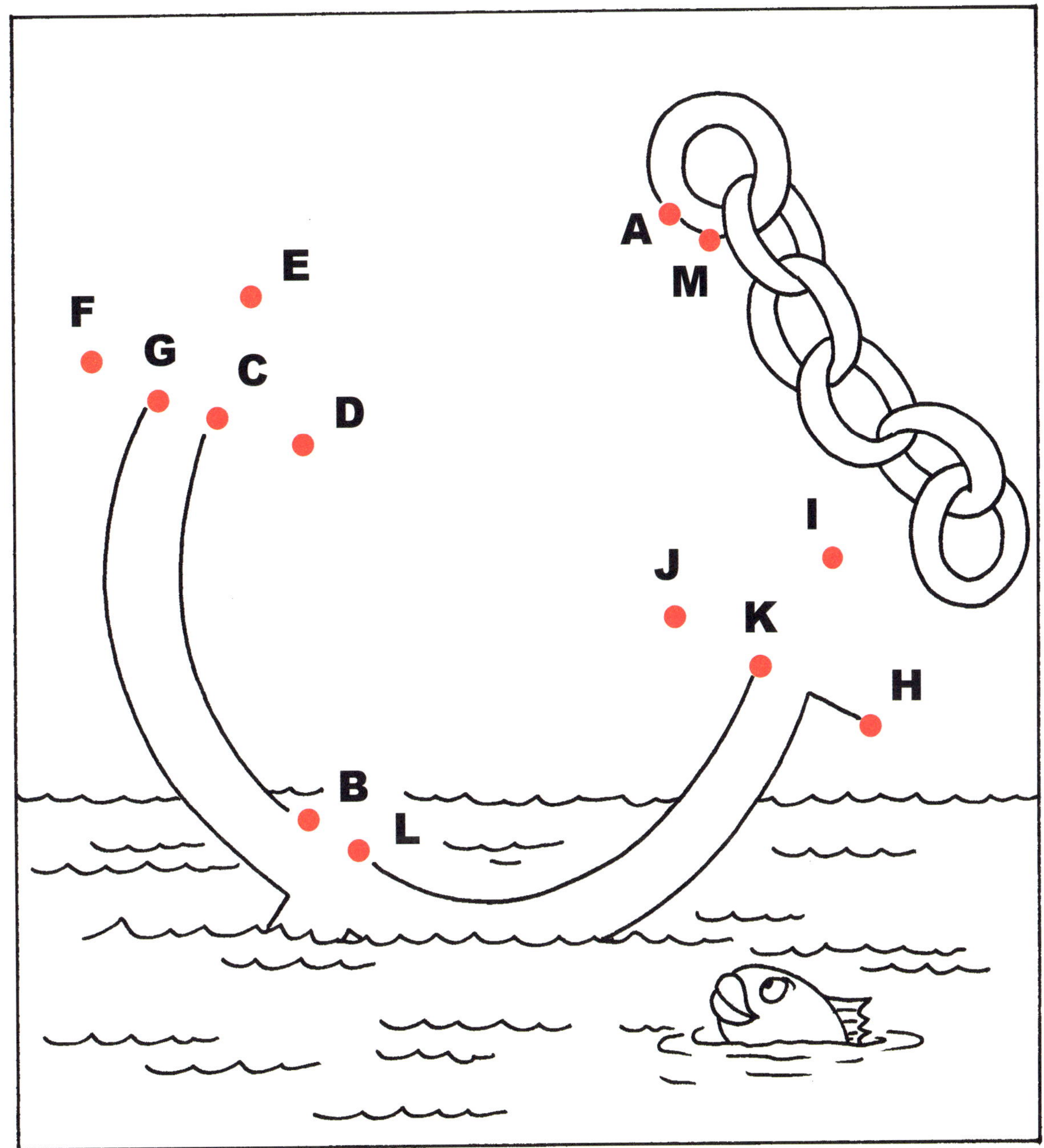

ABCDEFGHIJKLM

N is for Nutty Newt.

1 Trace and write.

2 Circle every **N**.

N N N Z T

H M J N N

How many? ____

Circle every **n**.

n n h n n

a n m o r

How many? ____

3 Add **n** and then say the word.

n ut

____est

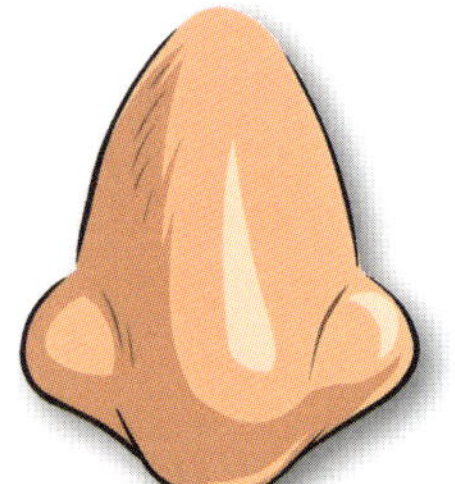

____ose

____eck

4 Circle the jigsaw parts that begin with **n**.

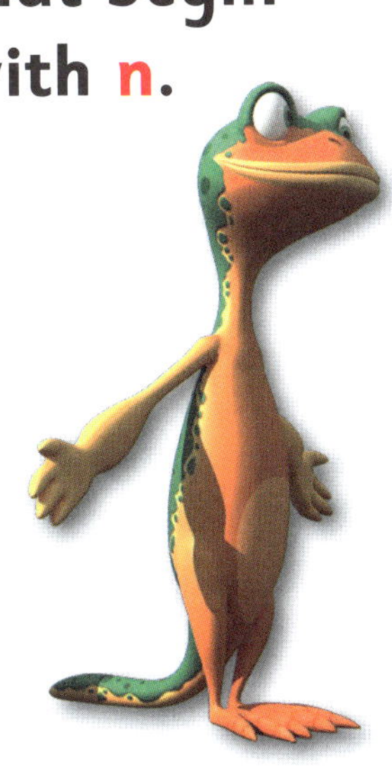

5 Match each letter to a picture.

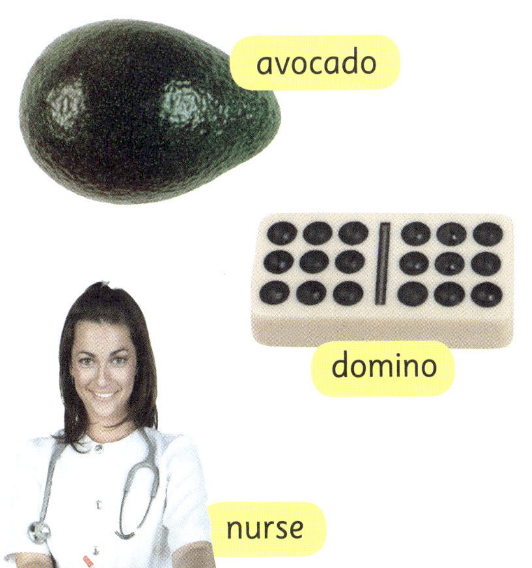

n

a

n

l

n

d

CHALLENGE

What number can you count to?

10 Good! 20 Great!! 100 Excellent!!!

1 Trace and write.

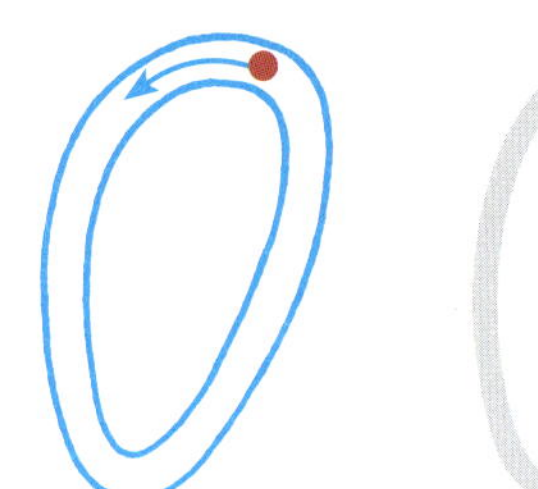

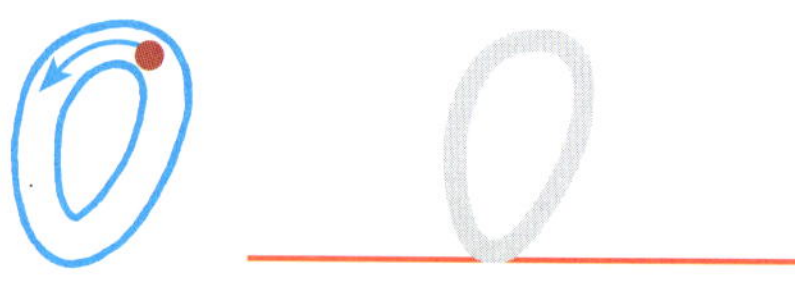

2 Circle every O.

O P C O O
O O D Q U

How many? ____

Circle every o.

o o a o e
b o c p o

How many? ____

3 Add o and then say the word.

____range

____ctopus

____tter

____nion

4 Circle all the oranges on the orange tree.

5 Match each letter to a picture.

o
f
o
c
o
g

CHALLENGE

How many orange things can you name?

3 Good! 5 Great!! 7 Excellent!!!

Pp

Peek a boo!
I'm Pinkipoo.

1 Trace and write.

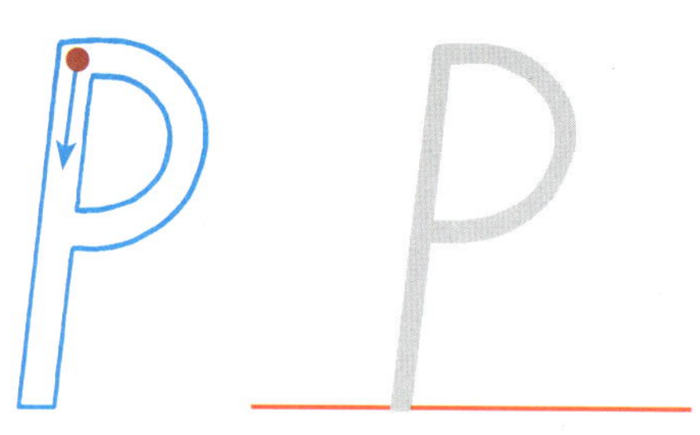

2 Circle every P.

P D P P B
P B P D P

How many? ____

Circle every p.

p p p b g
j b p a p

How many? ____

3 Add p and then say the word.

____eas

____enguin

____encil

____ear

4 Circle the pears that begin with p.

5 Match each letter to a picture.

p
m
p
j
p
l

CHALLENGE

How many pairs of socks?

Hello, I'm Queenie Quail.

1 Trace and write.

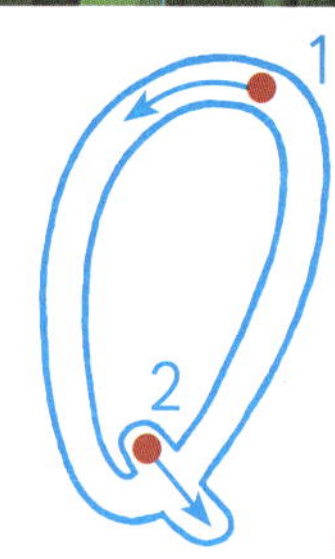

2 Circle every **Q**.

Q C Q E O

Q O D Q P

How many? ____

Circle every **q**.

q q 6 p t

a r q q b

How many? ____

3 Add **q** and then say the word.

q ueen

____ uail

____ uilt

____ uack

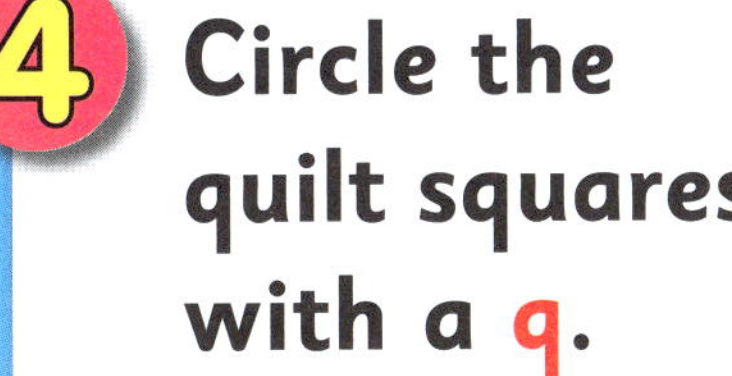

4 Circle the quilt squares with a q.

5 Match each letter to a picture.

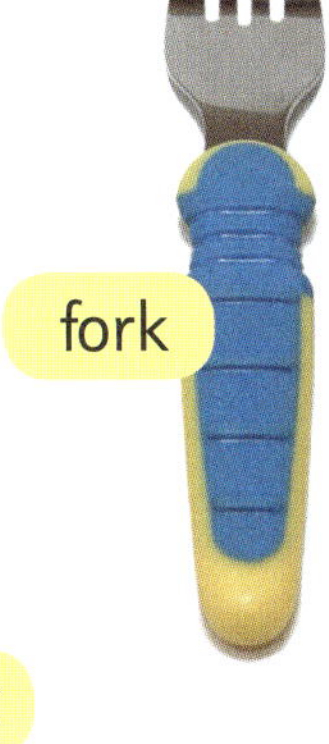

question mark

q
b
q
f
q
c

CHALLENGE

How many children in the queue?

Find the hidden pictures

Find each drawing in the picture.

Nn

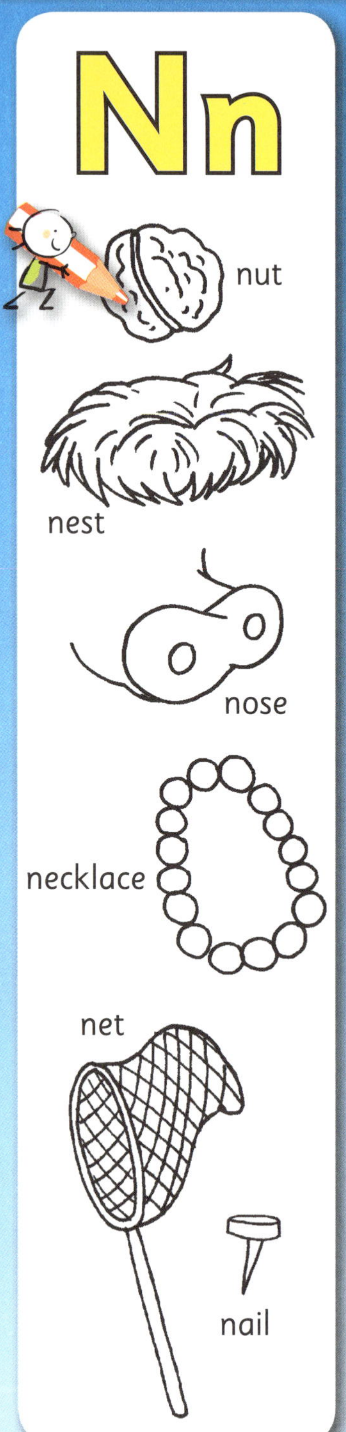

Oo

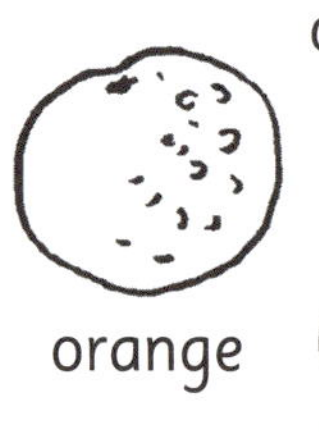

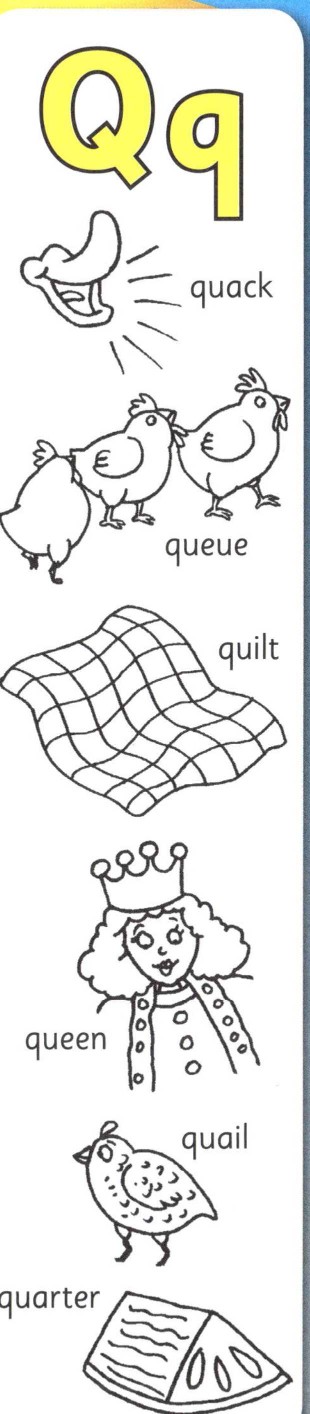
Qq
quack
queue
quilt
queen
quail
quarter

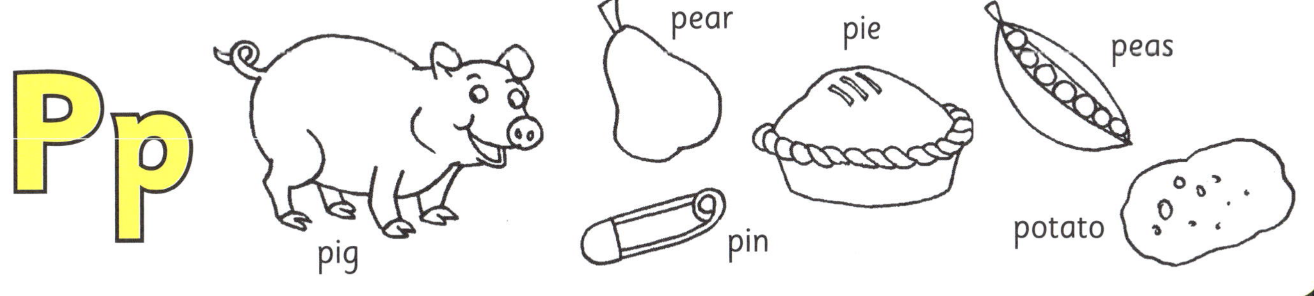
Pp
pig
pear
pie
pin
peas
potato

R is for Red Rabbit.

1 Trace and write.

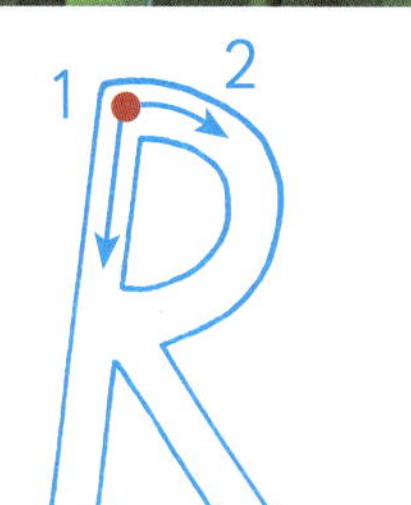

2 Circle every **R**.

R P A B R

T R R I A

How many? ____

Circle every **r**.

r r r g m

t i n r r

How many? ____

3 Add **r** and then say the word.

r ing

____ obot

____ abbit

____ ug

4 Circle the jigsaw parts that begin with r.

5 Match each letter to a picture.

CHALLENGE

How many red things can you name?

4 Good! 6 Great!! 10 Excellent!!!

Ss

Say hello to Sunny Snail!

1 Trace and write.

S S ______ s s ______

2 Circle every S.

S S S C S
J T S S U

How many? ____

Circle every s.

s s b c g
a r s s y

How many? ____

3 Add s and then say the word.

___un

___nail

___ix

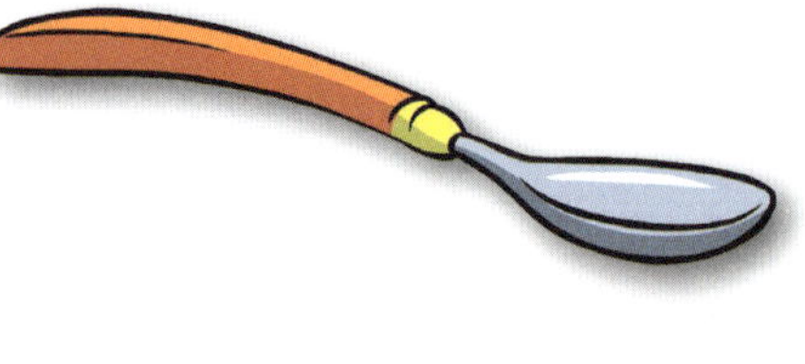

___poon

4 Circle all the strawberries that begin with s.

5 Match each letter to a picture.

CHALLENGE

Write 6 and 7.

6 6 6 7 7 7

Tt

Tiger Turtle is terrific!

1 Trace and write.

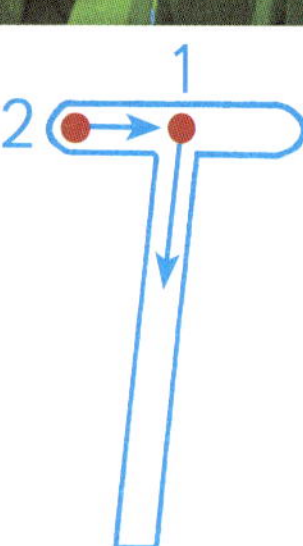

2 Circle every T.

T I V Z T
N T T E T

How many? ____

Circle every t.

t t h e b
i t l t t

How many? ____

3 Add t and then say the word.

____iger

____urtle

____ent

____ree

4 Circle the jigsaw parts that begin with t.

5 Match each letter to a picture.

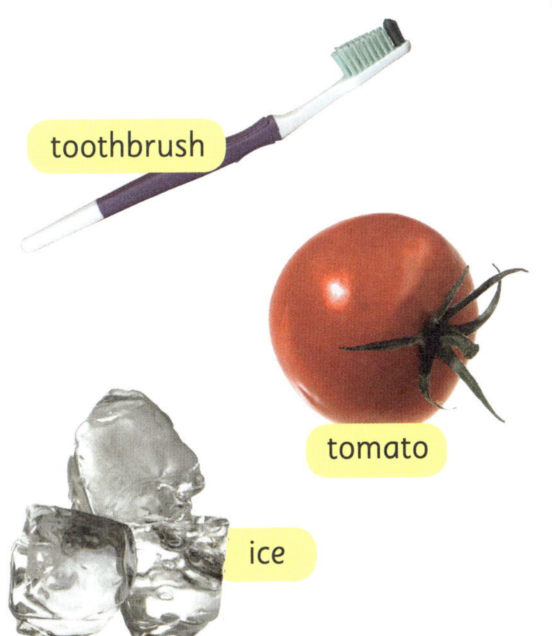

t
k
t
i
t
e

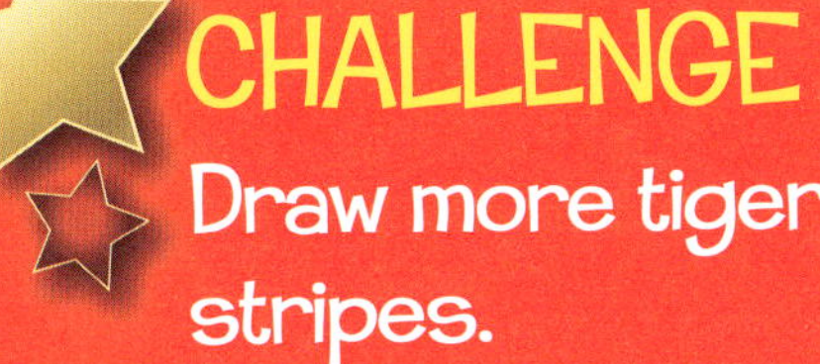

CHALLENGE

Draw more tiger stripes.

Uu

U is for Underting.

1 Trace and write.

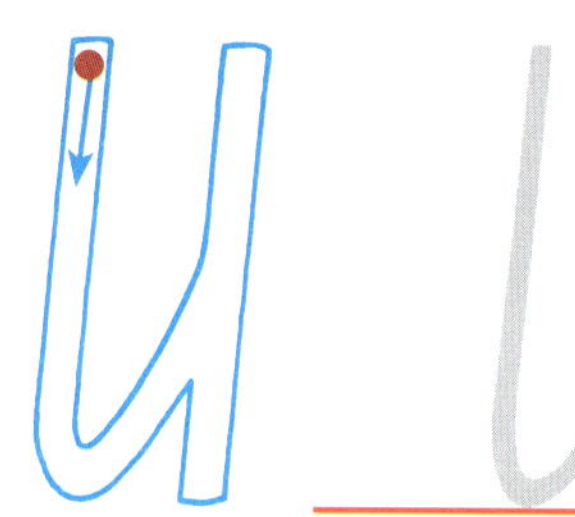

2 Circle every U.

U A V P U

S U U N O

How many? ____

Circle every u.

u i c n u

a u u m v

How many? ____

3 Add u and then say the word.

u mbrella

____gly

____nicorn

____nhappy

4 Circle all the u words.

5 Match each letter to a picture.

u
g
u
l
u
c

CHALLENGE

How many useful tools can you think of?

3 Good! 5 Great!! 10 Excellent!!!

Find the hidden pictures

Rr

rope

rhino

robot

ring

road

river

Find each drawing in the picture.

Ss

spider

snail

sail

sandwich

scarf

scooter

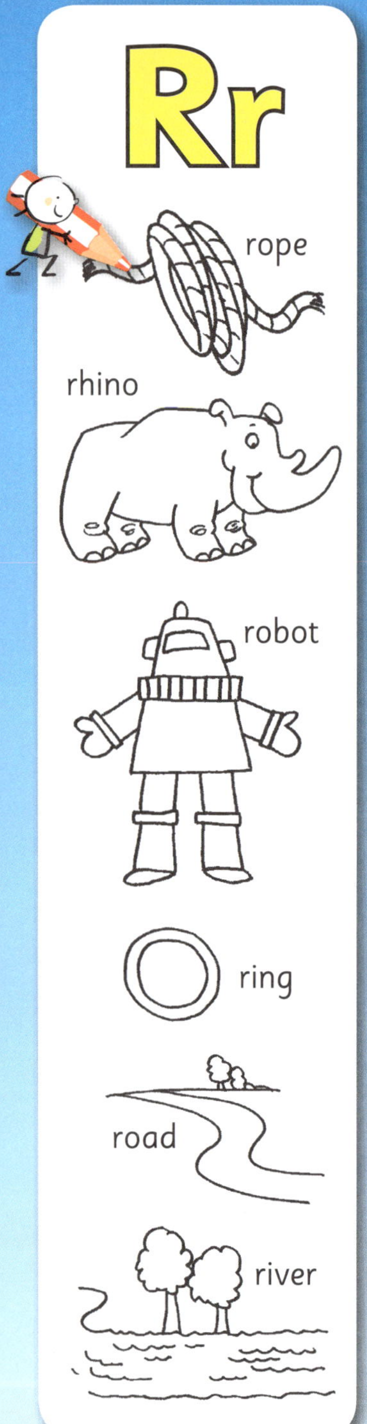

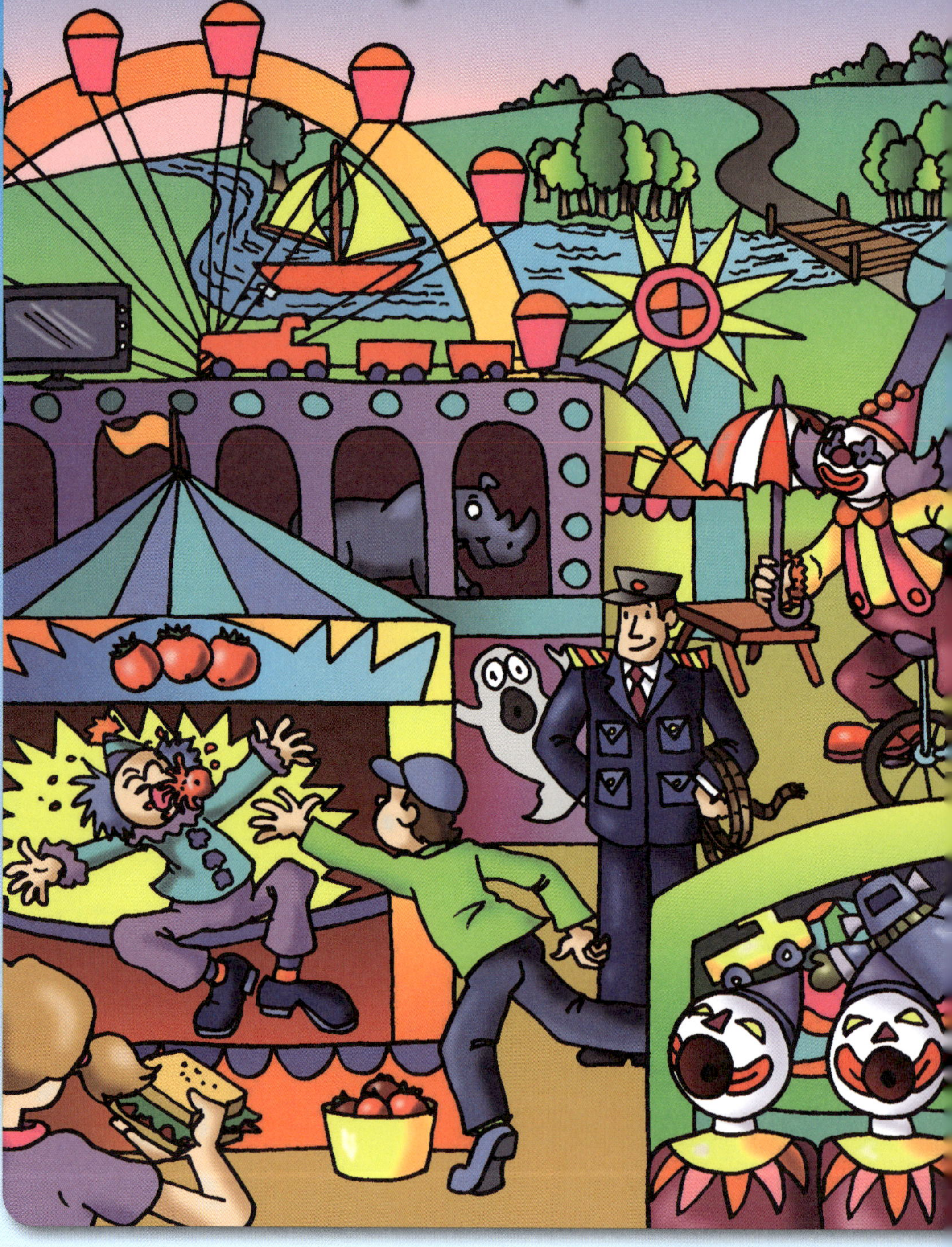

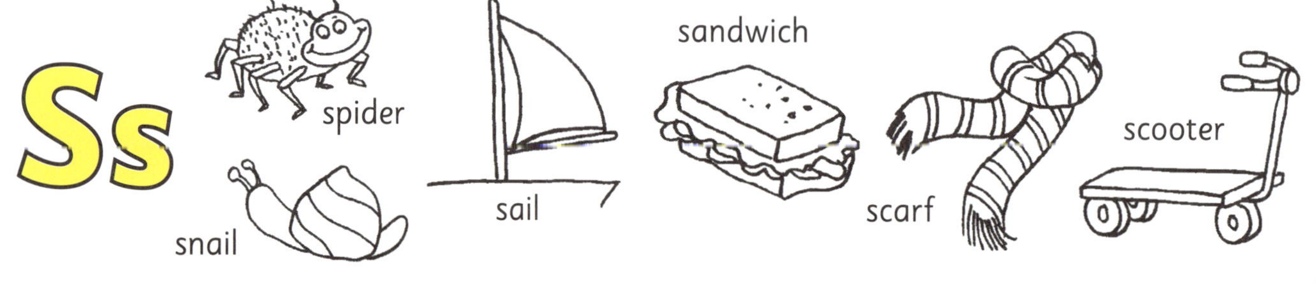

Uu
umbrella
unicorn
unhappy
uniform
unicycle

Tt
table
toy
tiger
tomato
television
tent

V is for Village Van.

1 **Trace and write.**

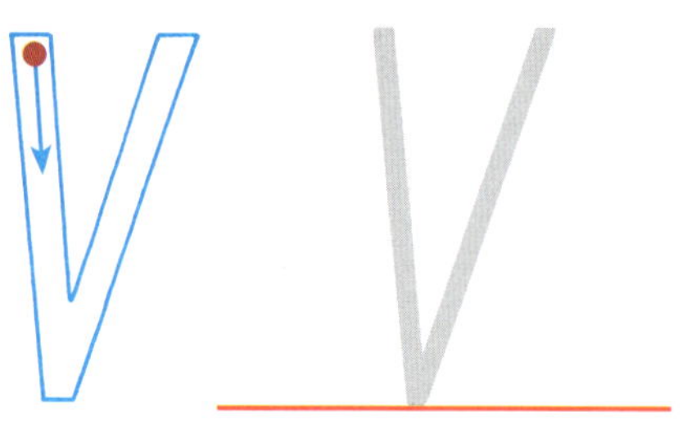

2 **Circle every V.**

V V U T E

L W V V T

How many? ____

Circle every v.

v v z v v

n v w t v

How many? ____

3 **Add v and then say the word.**

___et

___an

___iolin

___olcano

4 Circle all the vegetables.

5 Match each letter to a picture.

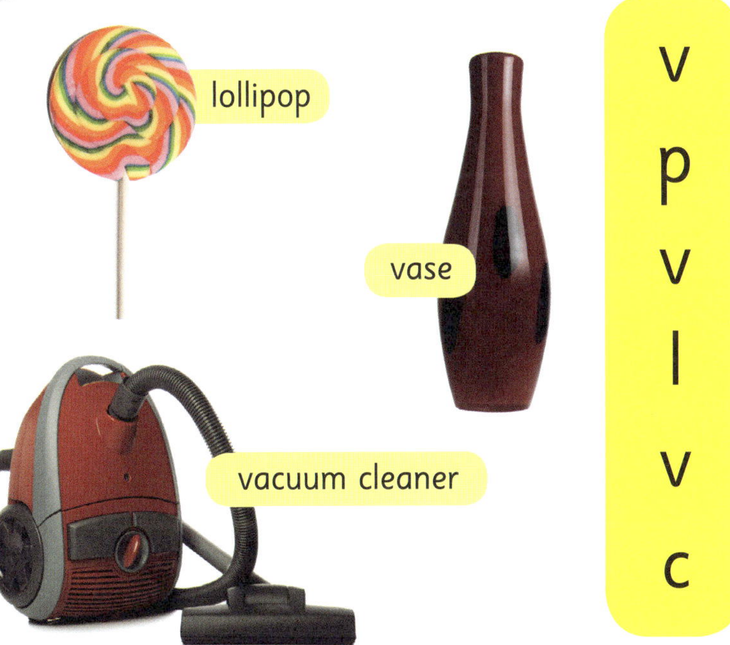

v
p
v
l
v
c

CHALLENGE

How many vegetables can you name?

5 Good! 8 Great!! 10 Excellent!!!

Wow!
It's Wheely Whale.

1 **Trace and write.**

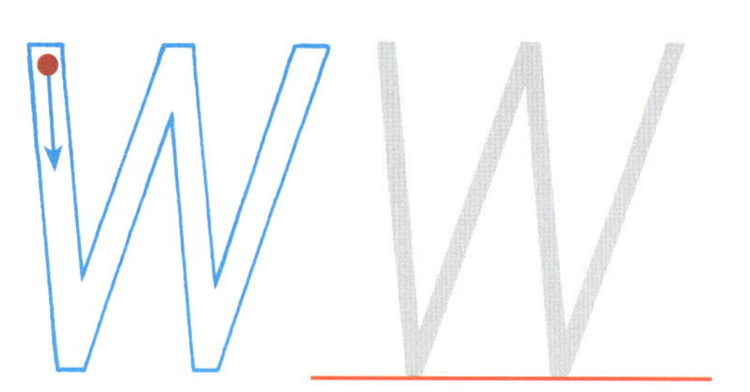

2 **Circle every W.**

W T W H E
A V W I W

How many? ____

Circle every w.

w w w n w
u v w o r

How many? ____

3 **Add w and then say the word.**

w eb

____ hale

____ in

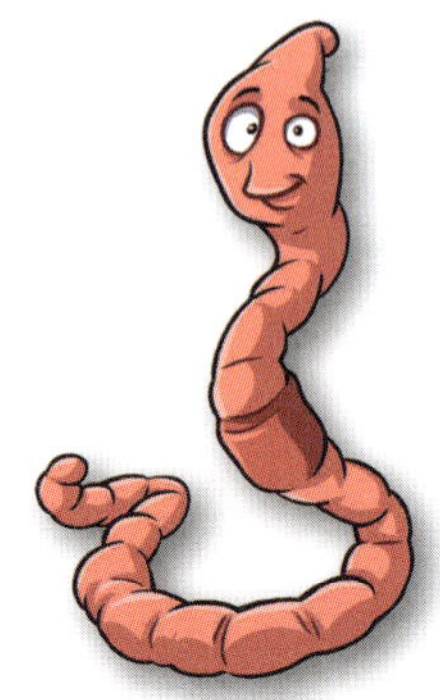

____ orm

4 Circle the web words that begin with w.

5 Match each letter to a picture.

w
s
w
r
w

CHALLENGE

Work your way through the maze. Can you win the prize?

Say hello to Xpanda!

1 Trace and write.

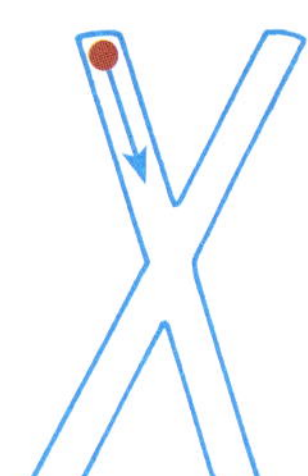

2 Circle every X.

X M I T X
L X X O X

How many? ____

Circle every x.

x x i x t
a x m x l

How many? ____

3 Add x and then say the word.

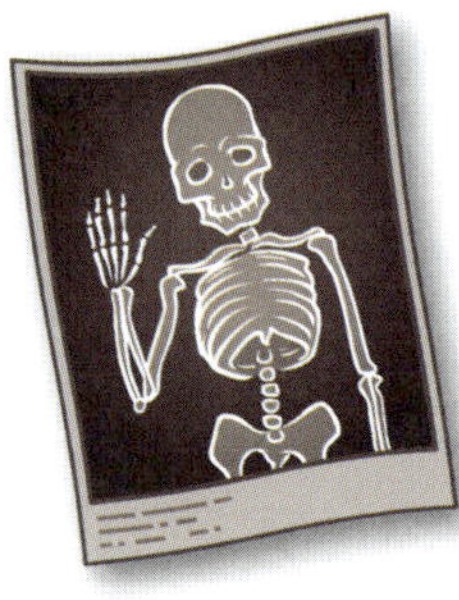

x -ray

si____

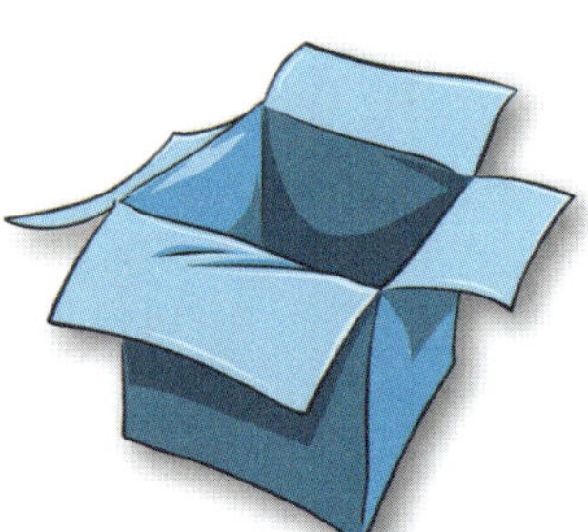

bo____

mi____

4 Put an x on every box.

5 Finish each word with an x.

wa____

ta____i

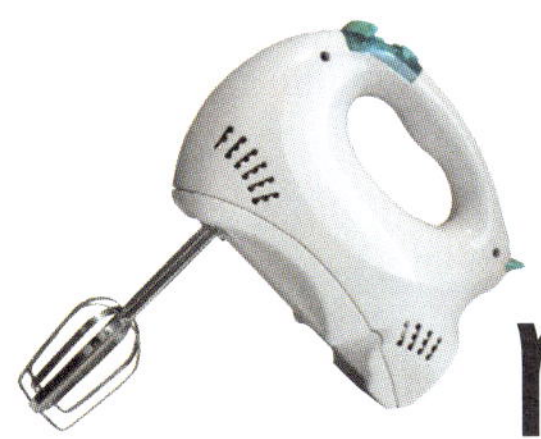

mi____er

e____it

CHALLENGE Complete the double zigzags.

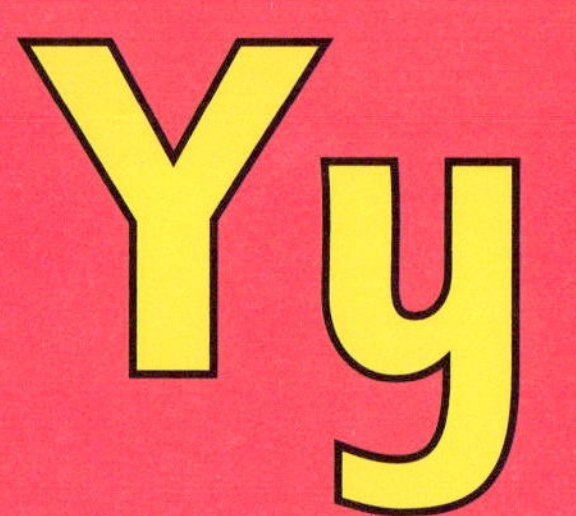

Yetiyo likes yoyos.

1 Trace and write.

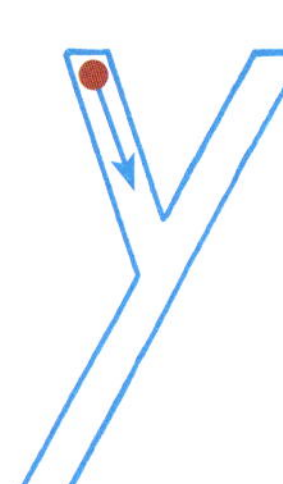

Y Y y y

2 Circle every Y.

Y W Y Y T
I H Y S Y

How many? ____

Circle every y.

y y g o y
o o y u y

How many? ____

3 Add y and then say the word.

y ellow

____ oyo

____ acht

____ uck

4 Circle the yellow flowers.
Draw some more.

5 Match each letter to a picture.

y
v
y
s
y
b

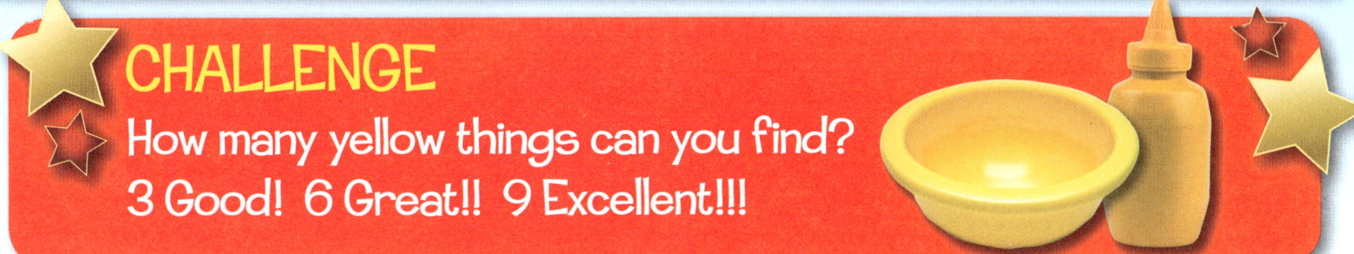

CHALLENGE

How many yellow things can you find?
3 Good! 6 Great!! 9 Excellent!!!

Zz

1 Trace and write.

Z Z z z

2 Circle every Z.

Z Z S Z P

N M Z I Z

How many? ____

Circle every z.

z m z t s

z p s z z

How many? ____

3 Add z and then say the word.

z ebra

____ oo

____ ap

____ oom

4 Draw more zigzags on the zebra.

5 Match each letter to a picture.

z
r
z
x
p
z

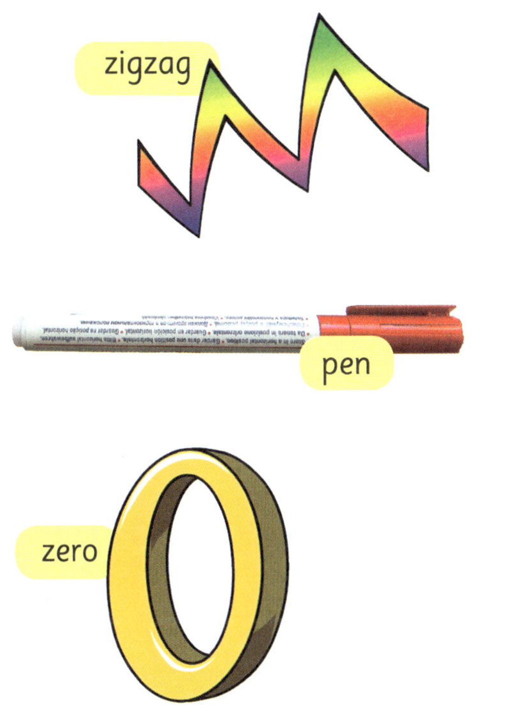

CHALLENGE

How many zoo animals can you name?

8 Good! 12 Great!! 15 Excellent!!!

Find the hidden pictures

Find each drawing in the picture.

Vv

vegetables

van

volcano

violin

vase

vacuum

Ww

web

worm

whistle

windmill

whale

waves

wand

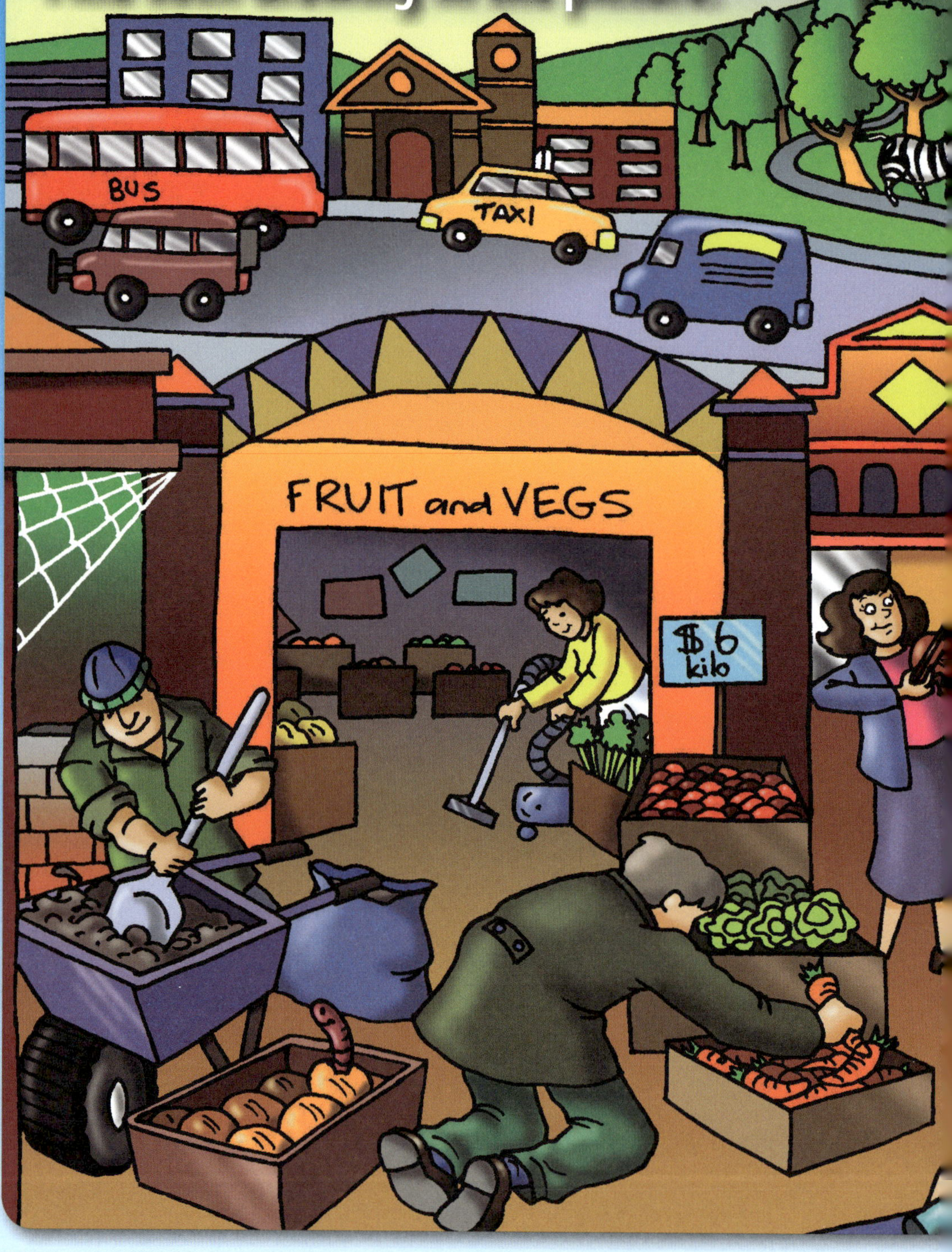

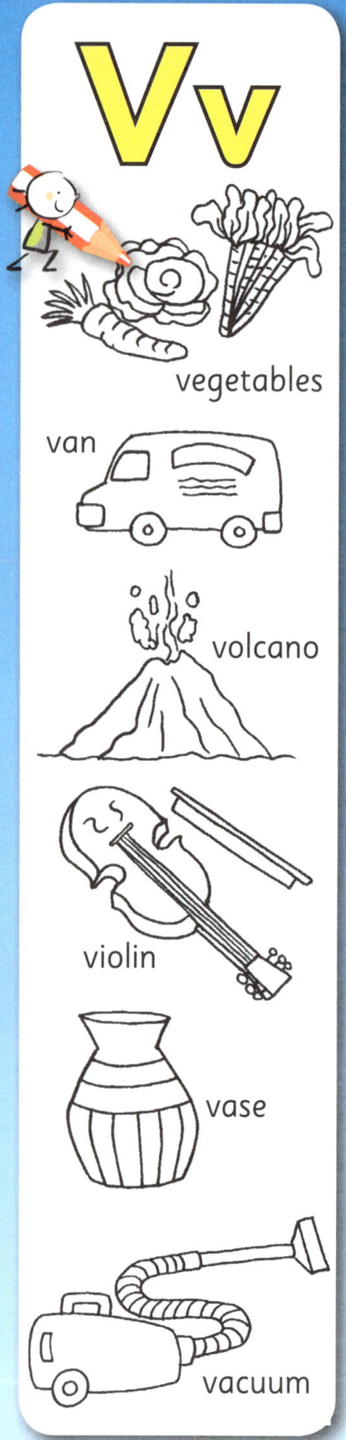

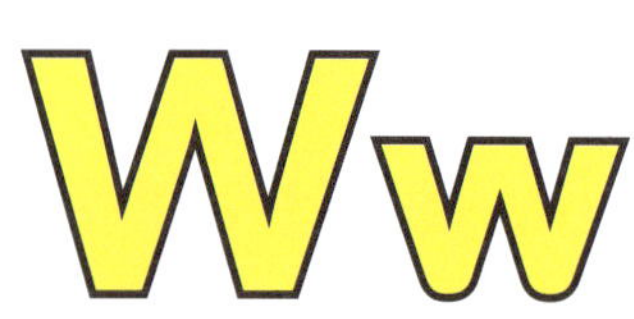

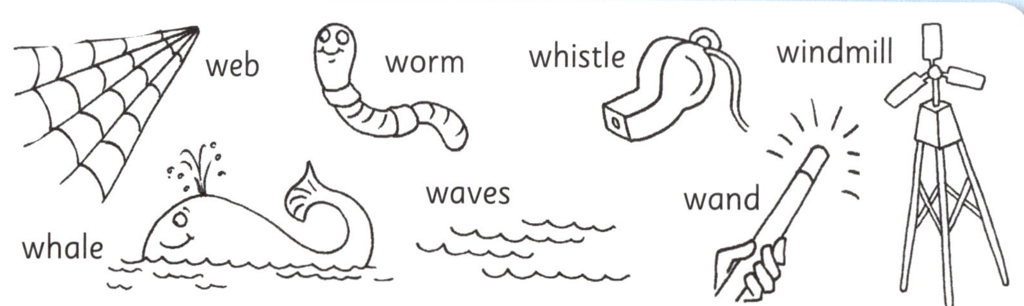

Zz
zigzag
zero
zebra

Yy
yoghurt
YOGHURT
yo-yo
yolk

Xx
x-ray
TAXI
TAXI
taxi
box
wax
six

Dot-to-dots

Connect the dots from n to z.

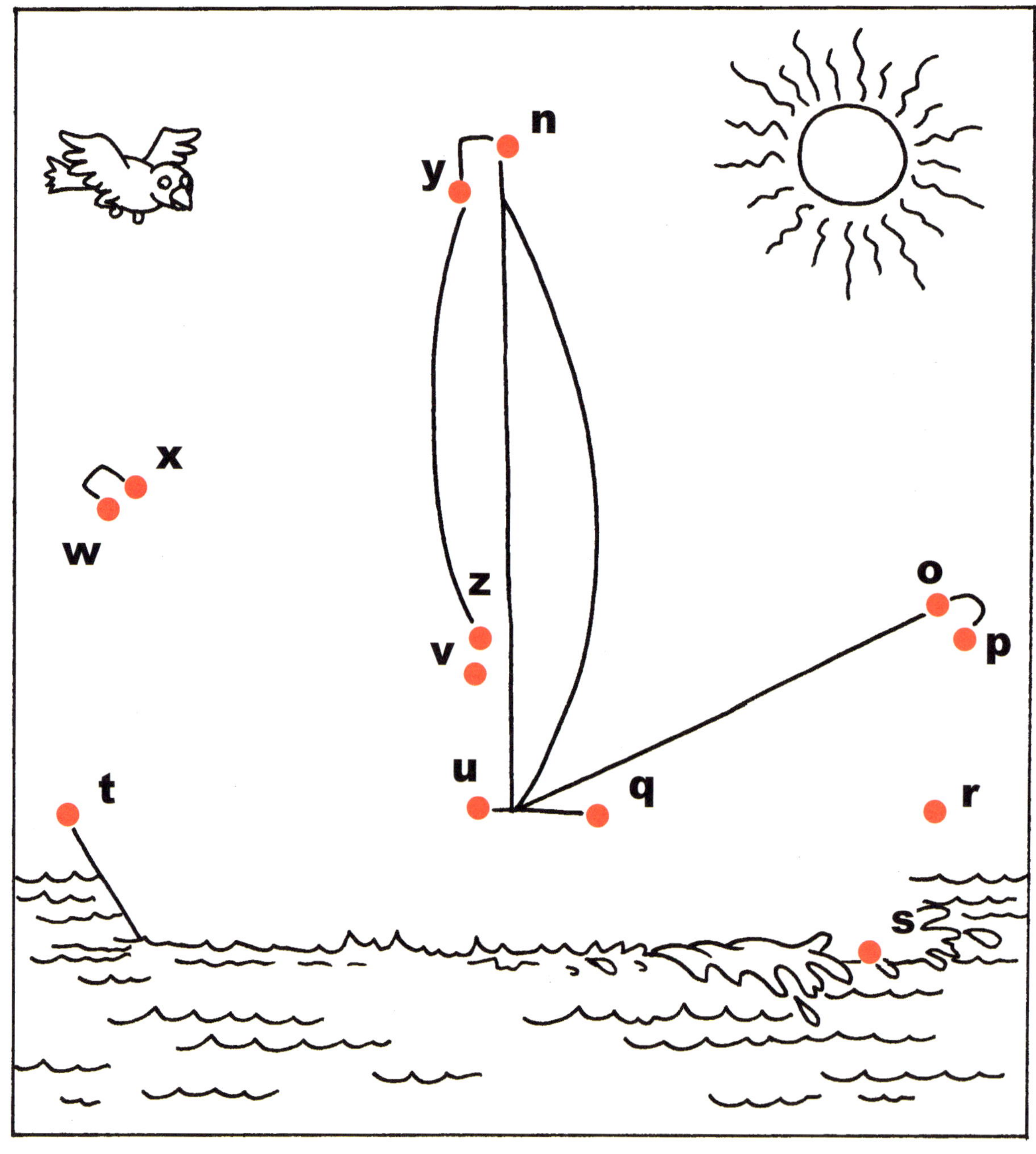

n o p q r s t u v w x y z

Connect the dots from N to Z.

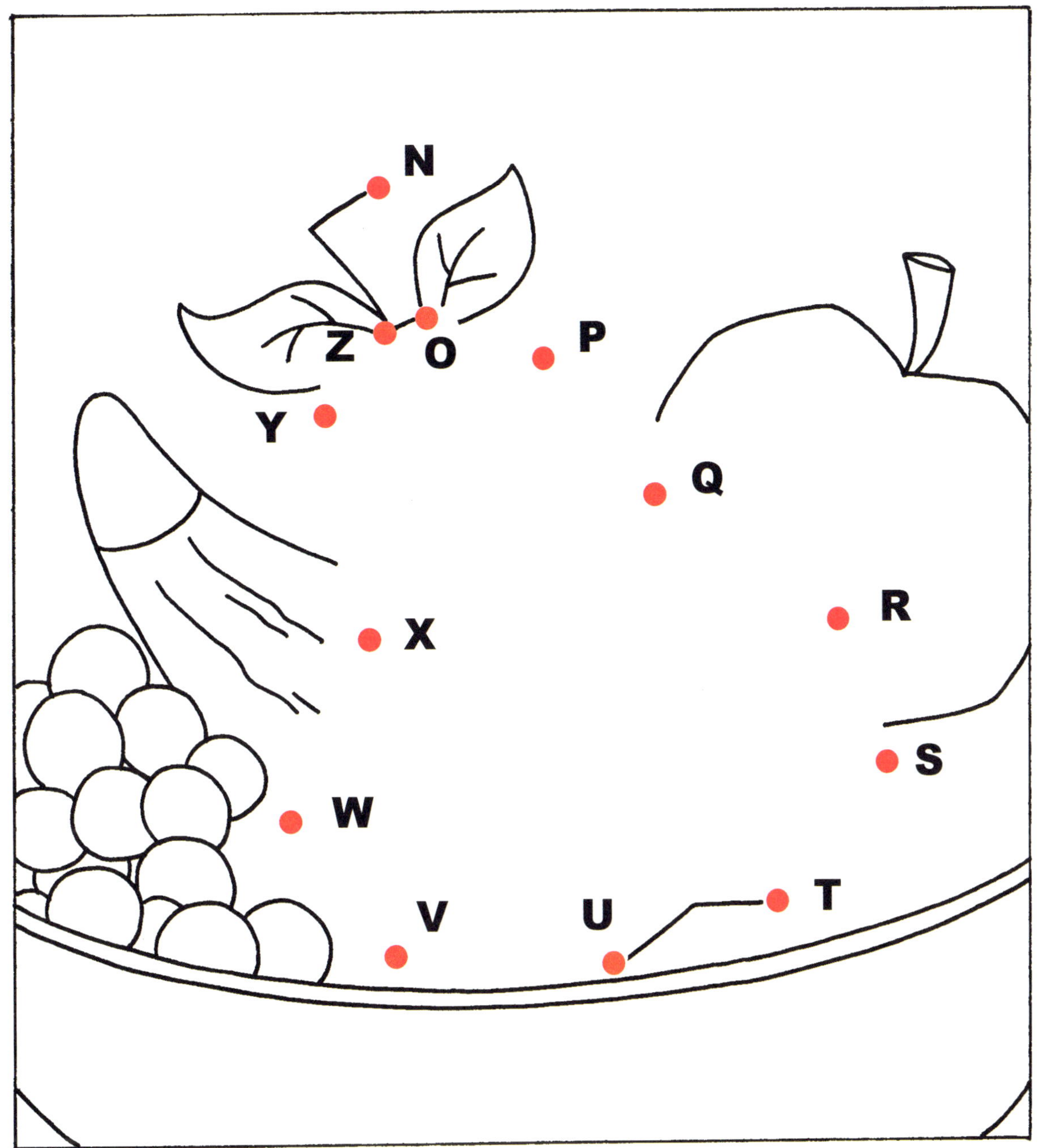

NOPQRSTUVWXYZ

Write the missing letters

A ___

___ b

C ___

___ g

H ___

___ i

M ___

___ n

O ___

___ s

T ___

___ u

___ y

___ d

E ___

___ f

J ___

___ k

L ___

___ p

Q ___

___ r

V ___

___ w

X ___

Z ___

Revision

Match each letter to its critter.

Oo
Nn
Qq
Pp
Rr
Tt
Ss
Uu
Ww
Vv
Xx
Zz
Yy
VILLAGEVAN
y

ABC
Reading
eggs
Congratulations!
You know
your alphabet!